PRAISE FOR DENVER MOON

"Take the Mars of *Total Recall*, the cybertech of *Ghost in the Shell*, the noir of *Blade Runner*, the action of *Cowboy Bebop*, and accelerate them to twelve times Earth escape velocity, then you will find yourself with the pure awesome joy that is *Denver Moon*."

—**MATTHEW KRESSEL**, multiple Nebula Award and World Fantasy Award finalist

"*Denver Moon: The Minds of Mars* combines *Blade Runner* and the original *Total Recall* with a dash of old-school detective noir that is hard to put down and leaves the reader wanting more."

—**INDIEREADER**

"This is Mars done as well as Elton John did it, as well as John Carpenter did it, as well as *Total Recall* did it. Move over, Andy Weir. Step aside, John Carter. Denver Moon is swaggering into this red landscape, and her footprints in the dust, they're going to last a few generations, I'd say."

—**STEPHEN GRAHAM JONES**, bestselling author of *Mongrels* and *Mapping the Interior*

"A searing mystery with a superlative, gun-toting protagonist."

—**KIRKUS REVIEWS** (Starred Review)

"*Denver Moon: The Minds of Mars* is noir sci-fi at its best. A powerful story that is hard to put down and highly recommended for mystery and sci-fi fans alike."

—**D. DONOVAN**, Sr. Reviewer, Midwest Book Review

"Crisp and compellingly told, *Denver Moon* is a high-tech, mystery-packed tale of our Mars-colonized tomorrow. Fans of Andy Weir and James S.A. Corey should take note."

—**JASON HELLER**, Hugo-winning editor and author of *Strange Stars*

"A tense story of a well-imagined Mars where belief is more powerful than a gun."

—**RICHARD KADREY**, bestselling author of *Metrophage* and the Sandman Slim series

"Enthralling action, a compelling mystery, and a uniquely gifted protagonist—all against the cyber-futuristic backdrop of a thoroughly bloodstained Mars. Denver Moon may be monochromatic, but by the time you're through with her hard-boiled, A.I.-powered adventure you will have seen every shade of red there is."

—**ALVARO ZINOS-AMARO**, Locus and Hugo Award finalist

"With a richly imagined and well-balanced mixture of Mickey Spillane and Philip K. Dick, the stories of Denver Moon deliver thought-provoking excitement, cunning twists, and deeply human characters (even the androids!). Put this on your must-read list."

—**CARTER WILSON**, *USA Today* bestselling author

"An Immersive kaleidoscope of futuristic treachery, mayhem, and murder."

—**MARIO ACEVEDO**, author of *Rescue from Planet Pleasure*

"This is one trip you have to take, from Martian fever to the ultimate fate of the human race."

—**ROBERT E. VARDEMAN**, author of *Darklight Pirates* and *God of War*

"A world where the boundaries between AI and humanity have blurred. A voyage destined to shape the fate of life on Mars. Full of unexpected twists, this excellent sci-fi narrative leaves you hungry for more."

—**JEANNE C. STEIN,** *New York Times* bestselling author

"This novella is recommended for all fans of speculative mysteries."

—**PUBLISHERS WEEKLY**

"...reminiscent of the original Total Recall: full of odd characters, dark passages and seedy levels of living beneath a harsh environment."

—**RT BOOK REVIEWS**

"This is cinematic science fiction, moving at a fast pace and building up a complex world."

—**CLARION REVIEWS**

"Gene-splice Raymond Chandler's mean streets with Leigh Brackett's Mars, weave in some slyly subversive thinking about AIs and religion and you'd be about at the place where *Denver Moon* starts. And it starts fast, then speeds up. A new noir take on a classic science fiction setting, populated with memorable characters, most of them less than nice. I hope we see more of Denver Moon."

—**KEITH FERRELL**, former editor-in-chief of OMNI Magazine.

"Readers looking for adrenaline-fueled and downright fun literary escapism should look no further than *Denver Moon*."

—**BLUEINK REVIEW** (Starred Review)

DENVER MOON

HEX PUBLISHERS

DENVER MOON

THE MINDS OF MARS

A NOVELLA

WARREN HAMMOND & JOSHUA VIOLA

DENVER MOON: THE MINDS OF MARS

and

DENVER MOON: METAMORPHOSIS

Copyedits by Matthew Wayne Selznick and Jennifer Melzer

Cover art by Kirk DouPonce
Denver Moon logo by James Viola
Interior art by Aaron Lovett
Typesets and formatting by Dustin Carpenter

A Hex Publishers Book

Published & Distributed by Hex Publishers, LLC
PO BOX 298
Erie, CO 80516

www.HexPublishers.com

Paperback ISBN-13: 978-0-9997736-6-6
Ebook ISBN-13: 978-0-9986667-3-0

First Hex Edition: 2018

10 9 8 7 6 5 4 3 2 1

Printed in the U.S.A.

For Dad, my greatest
teacher and friend.
—Josh

ACKNOWLEDGMENTS

THIS BOOK WOULD NOT BE POSSIBLE WITHOUT the support and assistance of Mario Acevedo, Keith Ferrell, Daniel George, Aaron Lovett, Mike McKibben, Jennifer Melzer, Jeremy Aaron Moore, James Rhodes, Matthew Wayne Selznick, Jeanne Stein, Carter Wilson, Dean Wyant, and Klayton.

Thank you,
Josh and Warren

PROLOGUE

HE CHECKED THE CLOCK.

Thirty minutes.

Only thirty more minutes.

He pulled on his gloves and twisted the metal rings to lock them to the sleeves of his suit. He turned the helmet over in his hands and watched the clock, watched the seconds pass. He'd been trapped there so long, all alone. Years had gone by. He was sure of it. But how many? Five? Ten?

How long had it been since he first opened his eyes and found himself in that room with stone walls? How long had he been wondering who he was? How he'd gotten here?

He tried so hard to piece it together, but the clues were scarce. That first day, the giant blood-caked bump on his head told him he'd suffered a major blow that must've taken his memory. A search of the one-room, hole-in-the-ground facility yielded no radios or phones. He'd found no computers or books or notes of any kind.

A single enviro-suit hung on the wall, and a ladder led to a cramped airlock above. He put on the suit and made his way up. Outside, he found himself standing upon a vast field of dirt and rock stretching from horizon to horizon. All his colorblind eyes saw were gray tones splashed across the landscape, but he knew right away where he was.

Mars.

But how? Why? Was he part of a research project? A colony? Where was everybody else? Were they coming for him? Or, Gods forbid, had he already missed a rendezvous he couldn't remember?

The days stretched into weeks, and the weeks into months, and the months into a dismal tedium where time no longer mattered. His diet was an unappetizing menu of freeze-dried rations and canned protein paste.

He figured out how to maintain the solar panels on the surface that provided his tiny facility with heat and electricity. He mastered the skills of producing breathable air using scrubbers that pulled elements from the atmosphere and mixed it with oxygen provided by the electrolysis of water.

To produce that water, he did the backbreaking work of carrying buckets of topsoil down the ladder to the extractor that took up almost a quarter of his living space. An hour later, the extractor would do the job of heating the dirt and capturing the frozen water molecules trapped inside, and then he'd lift the spent dirt back up the ladder to replace it with more freshly shoveled soil from the surface.

He explored the area, walking as far as his oxygen tanks would allow. In every direction, nothing but the desolate desert of Mars. He was marooned, and destined to starve to death when his supply of rations ran out.

But one day, when he went to the surface for his daily chores, he spotted a small, white dot in what he knew was a sea of red. The color white was as unnatural to the Martian terrain as a palm tree in Siberia, so he marched toward the spot until he found a pallet of supplies with a white parachute attached.

They—whoever they were—knew he was there, and over the years, they never forgot to make regular air drops. But he never saw who brought them.

The delivery was always the same. Twenty boxes of rations. A pair of replacement panels for the solar array. Replacement parts for all his equipment. A new enviro-suit in case his became damaged.

That was it. No messages or communications. No word of who they were, who he was or why he was here, or how long he'd have to remain.

Until yesterday.

Yesterday's delivery came with a note instead of supplies. The note consisted of three simple words. Pickup at noon.

Noon. Only fifteen minutes from now. He attached his helmet and climbed the ladder. He passed through the airlock and stepped outside for what he hoped would be his last time. He walked past the solar panels and found a spot to lay down on his back so he could see as much of the sky as possible.

He waited.

It started as a tiny speck that reflected the sunlight, and quickly grew to the size of a firefly. He sat up. Could it be? Could it finally be over?

The craft continued to approach, coasting silently across the wasteland he called home, the only home he could remember. His heart pounded in his chest. He stood and waved his arms and jumped up and down. This was it. He was finally leaving this prison never to come back.

His vision blurred with tears as the craft began to descend. It was a small ship, perhaps big enough for three or four people, though he could only see one pilot behind the windshield. A man, he thought, but he couldn't see more than that through the cloud of dust erupting all around him. The ship was right above him, a ladder descending from its belly. He hustled to get in position, his arms raised to grasp hold of the bottom rung.

The ladder came closer—one inch at a time—until it hovered just above his stretched hands.

With a loud clang, it changed direction and began to lift.

"Wait!" he shouted. "I'm not on!"

The ladder continued to rise. Rung by rung, it disappeared back inside the ship. He jumped for it, but even in Mars' reduced gravity he couldn't reach.

The hatch closed and the ship lifted upward. The nose of the craft turned around and it started back in the direction it came.

Despair forced him to his knees. He beat his helmet with his fists as he watched the craft shrink farther and farther away until it was gone.

CHAPTER ONE

I LOWERED THE VISOR OF MY HELMET, BUT IT wouldn't lock into place. I fiddled with the latch, then finally used a fist to knock it into position. A new helmet would be wise, but this was the helmet my grandfather gave me when I was a little girl. The helmet he gave me the day he died.

I cycled the airlock and stepped out into a long, sloped tunnel leading to the surface. My boots left deep prints in the sand the color of a dried bloodstain.

That was how most chose to describe the color of Mars. Bloodstained. Me, I couldn't see color. Call it a disability if you like, but I call it a gift. A gift that has kept me sane since taking the case. The things I'd seen, the carnage, the gore...

People I'd known all my life reduced to scraps scattered sloppily about like bits and pieces in a slaughterhouse.

Scene after scene, horror after horror, I thanked

my lying eyes for taking the edge off so much murder and death. It might not be much considering that, even in monochrome, the crime scenes were plenty vivid. Vivid enough to provide for several lifetimes worth of nightmares.

But at least it was something.

It was something.

At the end of the tunnel, I pushed my way through a series of heavy plastic flaps designed to keep out the worst of the dust and grit from Mars' constant sand storms. Shoving the last of the flaps aside, I was greeted by a gust of wind that made me adjust my footing to keep balance. Sand peppered my faceplate, and for the first time in a long time I was outside. The view was just how I remembered it. Dusty. Gloomy. Claustrophobic.

An arrow blinked brightly on the glass of my faceplate, and I angled in its direction. Stats flashed on screen, my eyes locking onto the distance to the habitat: 375.5 meters.

<Call them again, Smith.>

<I haven't stopped calling,> said my AI, his voice speaking directly into my mind. <They're not answering, Denver.>

Trusting my navigation system, I started into a slow loping jog, each step carrying me several feet thanks to the planet's weak gravity. My breath echoed loudly inside my helmet as the distance to the habitat ticked quickly downward.

<I hope they're okay,> said Smith. <You were like a daughter to them, you know?>

I knew. Yaozu and Aiwa Chen were among the very first group of settlers, a hundred of them in all, including my grandfather, who led the expedition along with Cole Hennessey. They were the reason I took the case—I couldn't trust another eye to stop the killer before this nightmare got to the Chens. I had to get to them first.

Smith said, <My sensors tell me there's a builder up ahead. You see it?>

Looking up, I could barely make the hulking outline of machinery through the haze of dust. Smith didn't live in my head, but he could see through my eyes. His vision was better in most ways than mine. I'd made a few enhancements since purchasing him, but not too many. He saw things down to the microscopic level, and if I were willing to spend the credits, Smith's vision could go submicroscopic. He could see colors, too, even though everything I saw remained one degree of gray or another. I'd tried neural devices and lenses, but none of them worked. Smith had the ability to colorize my vision, and on occasion I had the opportunity to view the world like everyone else, but thanks to the time lags, it came with a price: nausea, dizziness and Mars' worst migraine.

I veered to get around the space freighter-sized derelict, one of many littering the surface. Once used to carve a livable colony underground, builders like this one had been retired decades ago. Mars colony was as complete as it would ever be. At least until Jericho, the terraforming project, made the surface habitable…but that wouldn't be for another century or two.

I checked the display, less than fifteen meters to go. I stared straight ahead. Through the thick haze of the sandstorm, I could just make out the glow of a neon sign: *Marseum*. Under it was the word *Closed*.

I headed toward the light, and behind it, a flat surface began to emerge. A wall. Then, a roof. Finally, an airlock.

I pushed through the plastic flaps and didn't bother ringing the intercom before letting myself through the outer door. Shutting it behind me, I stabbed buttons with my gloved fingers until I heard the hiss of air filling the chamber and felt artificial gravity pushing down all around me. A minute later, the light turned on, and I popped my visor before spinning the hatch wheel until I heard the lock click.

<Be careful, Denver.>

Slowly, I pushed the door open and peeked my head through. "Yaozu? Aiwa?"

The museum was empty of people, the lights turned off except for those inside display cases. Cautiously, I moved through the room, past framed photos, and plaques, and mannequins in spacesuits. The next room was circular, the entire area painted a foreboding black. Detecting my presence, the holo-chamber lit, and I was on the surface thirty-five years ago when the sky was clear, and from what others used to tell me, the color of butterscotch.

I made for a holographic exit sign that led me out into a corridor. I passed through the lecture hall and glimpsed a tall figure moving quickly along the polished metal walls beside me. I reached for the weapon in the bag over my shoulder, but after a second look, I recognized the fringe of bleached-white hair swooping over Japanese features inside my enviro-helmet. Just my own reflection. I exhaled and made a quick check of the hall that yielded nobody. Up the stairs, I knocked on the door. "Yaozu? Aiwa?"

I pulled off my gloves and palmed the lockscreen. A light flashed, their home system still remembering me.

The living room was empty. Same for the bedroom and bathroom. But not the kitchen. There, on the table, centered on a plate, was an ear. A human ear.

<Here we go again,> said Smith.

My heart sank, and my eyes began to water. Not again. Eleven of the original settlers were already dead. All eleven in the last two days, and none closer to me and my long-deceased grandfather than Yaozu and Aiwa.

A trail of blood led to the back door. Beyond it, I knew, was the first habitat, the very first structure built on Mars. Part concrete bunker and part circus tent, it housed the original colony until the first of the tunnels were ready.

I slowly passed through the door, stepping into a

warehouse-sized structure that now protected and preserved the original habitat.

<You should be armed, Denver.>

<I am armed.>

<You know what I mean.>

<I won't draw until I have to. Like you said, Yaozu and Aiwa were like parents to me.>

<If they have the feve, you better be ready to draw fast.>

I moved toward the habitat. Overhead lights blinked in and out, causing ghostly shadows to flicker about. The blood spotted path pulled me forward. I passed a severed thumb without stopping to look. Stepped over the front half of a foot.

The habitat loomed large ahead of me. Two stories of concrete and steel. To the right stood the attached greenhouse tent, pitched of canvas and plastic that flapped slowly in the breeze created by giant ventilation fans in the warehouse ceiling.

The habitat airlock was open. Inside, a donation jar containing a handful of credits sat on a pedestal.

<I'm picking up a biological heat signature,> Smith said.

<Just one?>

<Yes.>

<Where?>

<In the habitat. Near my old office.>

<You know I hate when you call it *your* office.>

<Sorry, Denver, but *you* know that's how *I* think of it.>

I gritted my teeth. If he wanted to believe he really *was* my grandfather instead of an AI who had simply been updated to include my grandfather's memories, now wasn't the time to argue.

I turned left, then right, and stopped in my tracks. A body lay on the ground. Naked. The head was missing, and his gut had been split, organs yanked free and left in a pile. He was male, and the tattoo on his shoulder — a simple gray circle representing Mars — told me this was Yaozu.

I swallowed the lump in my throat and blinked away the tears forming in my eyes before moving past. Smith had detected a heat signature in the next room. Aiwa was still alive. Maybe it wasn't too late.

The door was cracked and I used a boot to push it open. Aiwa was inside, standing in the corner, her platinum hair matted with blood. In her hands was her husband's head, one of his cheeks marred by teeth marks, the other cheek missing as if eaten.

"Aiwa," I said, "it's me, Denver."

Her eyes didn't register my presence. Instead, they darted madly about the room.

"Red fever has you," I said. "I can help. Let's get you to a doctor, understand?"

She lifted the head like she was going to take another bite, but then she let it drop from her hands. Yaozu's head landed with a thud and rolled a few inches to the side.

"That's right," I said. I reached into the bag strapped over my shoulder and pushed past my gun to the syringe underneath. "Let me give you this shot, and we'll get you the care you need."

She didn't look my way. Instead, her eyes landed on a bloody butcher knife resting on the floor.

"Stay with me," I said before I bit off the cap of the syringe and spit it to the floor. "Whatever's in your head, it's just the feve talking. I'm going to take it all away, okay?" I reached back into my bag and pulled out a small vial of charcoal liquid. "This is just a sedative. It's going to take all your pain away."

I filled the syringe. Aiwa's head cocked to the side like an animal watching something it couldn't understand. I took a slow step toward her, my hands raised to not appear threatening. She was just two meters away. "You're doing good, Aiwa, just stay still."

<Um, Denver,> said Smith, <I hate to interrupt.>

<Then don't.>

<But I just got a message, one I think you're going to want to hear.>

I took another step forward. <The message can wait.>

<But it's from your grandfather.>

For a split-second, I froze. Then I shook off the ridiculous comment and continued toward Aiwa.

<He's dead, Smith.>

<I know, but the message was buried in my…his

memories. I thought it was garbage code, but it just unencrypted itself.>

I stepped closer, keeping Aiwa trapped in the corner. <I'm a little busy right now.>

<But your grand—>

<Shut up, dammit!>

Aiwa scratched her head. I winced at the sound of her fingernails rasping against her skull. A trickle of blood leaked from her hairline to a forehead wrinkle and flowed toward her ear.

"That's right," I said. "Just relax, and it will all be over soon."

A chime sounded, and a hologram lit above Aiwa's desk. As if by reflex, she turned to it. I glanced at the image myself, my jaw dropping at what I saw. It was Ojiisan. My grandfather who died twenty years ago.

<See?> said Smith. <It looks like Aiwa got the same message you did.>

My grandfather was dead. Yet there he was, clear as day. Ojiisan hadn't aged a bit since I'd last seen him when I was a girl. The black hair by his temples was still shot with gray. His chin stood proud and his eyes held a firm gaze. His mouth began to move, but I couldn't hear his voice. The volume was too low.

How could he have sent a message after all these years? It didn't make any sense. I took a tentative step toward the desk, and like a flash, Aiwa slipped out from the corner, an elbow catching me as she darted past my position. I spun around, but she already had the knife. She charged, her eyes seized by madness. I dodged, but not fast enough, and felt the blade penetrate my suit and bite into my side.

I stuck her with the needle, sinking it hard into her shoulder, and stabbed the plunger down.

She took another swing. I ducked low, managing to avoid the blow. I ran for cover behind the desk, but she came over the top, her weight slamming me across the chest. I fell into the wall and lost my balance, landing painfully on my hip. She dropped on top of me, a knee pinning me to the floor.

I grabbed the wrist holding the knife with both of my hands and tried to turn the blade away from my chest but, despite Aiwa's age, I was powerless to stop the edge from slowly sinking closer to my body. I let out a long breath in hopes of compressing my chest, but it wasn't enough and the blade's tip dug painfully into my breastbone.

"Aiwa! Please! It's me. It's Denver!"

She couldn't hear me. My words were just background noise in a head overcome with the feve. Her face was flushed, veins straining under her skin. Her lips were stretched wide to bare every single tooth in her mouth. The blade sunk deeper. My arms shook under the pressure.

I heard a bone snap in her wrist, but still, the feve

wouldn't release its hold on her. She raked me with her other hand, nails digging into my cheek like a cat's claws.

I managed to stabilize the knife, and with a concerted push, moved it upward and away from my body. I was winning the battle now as the drug took effect. Summoning what little energy I had left, I rolled her off me. The knife fell from her hand and she finally went slack.

I stood on wobbly knees. Blood ran from my gouged cheek. My suit was wet from the wounds in my side and chest.

I looked at the desk, at the hologram of Ojiisan, his mouth still moving as he impossibly delivered a message from the grave.

I walked to the desk and turned up the volume.

Mars is in grave danger. You must find me.

CHAPTER TWO

I WALKED OUT OF THE PSYCHIATRIC WARD AND breathed deep to clear my head of the smell of antiseptic. Dropping down a set of poorly lit stairs, I headed for Red Tunnel.

Two weeks had passed since I saved Aiwa. Seeing her confined to a straightjacket, jerking incessantly against her restraints, I wondered if I should've saved her at all.

Red fever was a scourge. A plague that destroyed families and lives. There was no cure. Once you had it, you had it.

The lucky ones would have a hot-tempered episode or two, and that would be the worst of it. The unlucky ones entered an unstoppable rage at the smallest provocation. Others slipped into a fugue state, waking an hour later covered in blood and surrounded by mutilated bodies.

Then there were cases like Aiwa's. A complete loss. An empty husk of a human whose soul had been purged in favor of the ravings of a lunatic.

I turned into a narrow alleyway. Visitors always struggled to find their way around the maze that was Mars City, but I knew where I was going. I was a native, a member of the first generation of true Martians.

Before us came the colonists. Led by Ojiisan and his partner Cole Hennessey, they used the diggers to create this intricate network of tunnels, wide and deep enough to support equipment bays, factories, schools, and residences. All the space we needed to house a large population of workers and immigrants.

The ultra-wealthy lived in the luxury domes above. The rest of us lived underground. Mars City and most of its supporting installations and communities were located in the top fourteen levs. Below that, less legitimate, or less officially sanctioned facilities and businesses ran rampant.

I rounded another corner. A man blocked the exit. Curled up in a ball, he rocked back and forth and clawed lines into his own face. Definitely the feve. The closer you got to Red Tunnel, the more you saw that sort of thing.

<Careful, Denver,> Smith said.

I darted past the man and climbed a long ramp that turned right into the main thoroughfare. Red Tunnel was eighteen levs below the surface. The tunnel was long and straight, the ceiling carved smooth. Steel tracks ran down the center, once used to cart massive quantities of stone.

I looked down the street past a group holding *FIGHT*

THE FEVE and *SHIELD YOUR MIND* signs and noticed a small crowd gathering around a tent stocked full of coolers. Organ peddlers weren't uncommon down here. Most sold the usual stuff: hearts, livers, kidneys. Some even offered android and botsie parts, too. But this tent's signage indicated a very different spread of body parts: the alien variety.

I'd encountered the same thing while working a case a few years back. The vendors lured customers with the promise of extending our short Martian lifespan by a few extra years. And, if you were lucky, you could be cured of the feve, too. All for the price of a six-course meal up in the domes. A scam, no doubt, but there were plenty of people in the tunnel gullible enough to believe in aliens and willing to throw their hard-earned credits at a fantasy.

I passed a small grocery and an electronics shop. The neon signs and industrial cables hanging from over-crowded buildings made the place look like some circus in the deepest recesses of hell, but it was actually one of the nicer neighborhoods. No pharmapits or murder-sim houses. No botsie parlors or rip shows. The area was decent for families—as decent as it could be down here—at least for those who weren't rich enough to afford a home a few levs above.

A shopkeeper cleaned the walk outside her shop with a suction unit, working up a small cloud of dust. I veered to avoid the worst of it. The dust was a constant annoyance, a symptom of the terraforming project. No matter how hard we tried, we couldn't keep it out of our air supply, at least not when sandstorms were pummeling the surface, which was pretty much always.

<Twenty-minute warning,> said Smith.

<Got it.> I'd come down here because I was due to meet Cole Hennessey, the Founder and Peerless Leader of the Church of Mars, at the main temple. After two weeks of trying, I'd finally gotten a response this morning when his assistant set me up for an appointment.

If anybody could make sense of my grandfather's message, it would be him. Whether I could trust a word he said was another story, but seeing past the bullshit was what I did for a living. He and my grandfather were partners once. Best of friends, but they became adversaries. Why, I never knew, but the divisions ran deep.

Even the original hundred colonizers seemed to have little idea what came between them. I'd tracked down quite a few of them over the last two weeks, those still alive, anyway. A total of eleven perished when the crisis struck, all of them suddenly ravaged by the fever. How the feve could strike in such a seemingly coordinated fashion, I didn't know. But such strangeness had happened before.

Red fever was the mystery to end all mysteries. Nobody knew how it was transmitted or why it affected some worse than others. Some thought we'd awoken an alien organism buried in the rocks of Mars. Others said it had been sent by the gods to punish us for not being proper stewards of Earth.

Most thought it wasn't a disease at all. It was the red. All day, every day, all you saw was red. Red rock. Red dirt. The floor. The ceiling. The walls. All of it coated in a dusty, red film. Even the air we breathed took on a red hue. It was the red that drove you mad.

This was a theory enhanced by the fact that those of us who were colorblind were immune. For a while, it had been fashionable for people to use color-correcting lenses and glasses. Some of the wealthy even swapped out their eyes for monochromatic synthetics, but the popularity didn't last long. Not after the replacement eyes had been proven to be of no consequence when it came to the feve. For some reason, you had to be born colorblind.

Like I said, a mystery to end all mysteries. One thing we did know was the feve was localized to Mars. There hadn't been a single case contracted on Earth or Luna or any of the space stations. The feve was purely Martian, as if Mars itself was contagious.

Hell of a slap in the face that must've been. The colonizers came to build a new world, one that was better than the dying Earth they fled. Those early years were a time of hope, a time to be proud of humanity.

But then came the feve.

It didn't stop us from terraforming. As Earth continued to decline, humanity had no other choice. But the thought of Mars being our savior—a paradise for the future generations—had been permanently dashed. Life on Mars would always be a wretched existence filled with violence and paranoia. Like those stories in the Christian Bible had come true. We'd sinned and been sentenced to this red hell.

A neon sign blinked the words *Church of Mars*. The temple was the church's main headquarters, but there were plenty of other shrines spread across Mars City. They set up shop down there because they believed the tunnel needed their message most of all. I turned into a broad corridor with a low ceiling. Powerful lights hidden behind stone pillars bathed the area in warm tones. To the right was a small shack. Through the windows I saw recruits getting their heads shaved and foreheads tattooed with a white circle that represented a Mars free of red fever. Others were being fitted for white robes. All of them were about to devote their lives as monks to the church.

I approached a steep incline. The right side was cut by stairs while the left side was not. I remembered the first time I saw the ramp when I was a young girl. I thought it was for wheelchairs, although I should've known the incline was far too severe. And why was the ramp's surface covered in bumps that stood from the flat surface like an egg from a carton? Wouldn't those bumps make it hard to push a wheelchair?

"It's about discipline," said Ojiisan. "The Church of

Mars believes rigid self-control is the only way to manage the feve."

I didn't understand what my grandfather meant until I saw my first robed monk crawling up the ramp. I remembered standing next to her, on these very stairs, and watching her tortured face. I'd never seen a face like that before. I saw the tears streaming from her eyes, her lips curled in agony. I remembered the way she lifted one knee at a time only to settle it back down in fresh misery. Her skin was so drained of color even *my* eyes could see the full weight of her suffering.

How could anybody subject themselves to such torture? Could the feve be that bad?

The answer was yes. A fact that made the church more and more powerful every day. The bargain was simple: Give your life to them, and they'll teach you the skills you need to control the fever. Whether they could really deliver on that promise was up for debate.

A large school of thought believed the Church of Mars was a response to the first and worst of the red fever epidemics, but I belonged to a much smaller and more radical school. I thought the Church of Mars and all the harshness of belief and condemnation it rested upon was itself a symptom of the feve. A sickness. A disease. A plague. Just a more socially acceptable one than running through the streets screaming and pillaging and killing.

Socially acceptable to some. Mainly those who caught the CoM fever.

Fifty stairs up, my lungs were straining hard. I took a break at one hundred stairs, the midway point. There was no other way up to the church. No elevators or escalators. Even the Peerless Leader himself made the same trek at least once a day, always using the stairs save for the one day a year all adherents, himself included, had to crawl the ramp.

Near the top, I offered a monk a few words of encouragement. All he could manage in response was a mournful moan. The barcode on the back of his hand told me he'd been in prison. The jails were ripe territory for church recruits.

I climbed the last stair and wiped sweat from my brow. The space out front of the church was broad enough to hold a large crowd. Above the doors was a small balcony just big enough to hold a single priest. Before entering, I knew I had to check my weapon, but when I went to the window to pass the Smith & Wesson over, the man behind the counter waved me off.

"Go on in, Ms. Moon," he said. "We've been expecting you."

CHAPTER THREE

RE-HOLSTERING THE GUN, I WENT TO THE TALL carved wood doors that had been salvaged from a mosque in Istanbul before the city went underwater.

Pulling on a heavy iron ring, I let myself inside and sucked in a breath. No matter how many times I'd been there, the sight before me never failed to awe. Walls of intricately carved stone seemed to stretch all the way into space. Somewhere up there was a clear glass ceiling, a window to heaven itself, according to Peerless Leader Cole Hennessey. On the rare clear day, you really could see the stars. On days marred by sandstorms, holographic imagery completed the illusion.

Down at the bottom, turquoise and emerald lights shined from every possible angle. Although the color itself was lost on me, I knew the intent was to drown out every ounce of red from the spectrum. Cast in aquamarine, many thought the church looked like it was peacefully underwater.

Straight ahead was the altar. The simple podium appeared to float upon a cloud of smoke that made the whole church smell of incense. Worshippers knelt on polished stone floors. To the right and left were domed carve-out rooms for meditation. Tight geometric patterns adorned every surface.

The sound of footsteps came my way and I turned to find a robed woman approaching. "This way, Ms. Moon."

I followed her out a door that led down to a warren of tunnels below the church. Leading me through a disorienting series of turns, we finally arrived at an open door. Cole Hennessey sat at a desk inside.

He looked up from a thick, leather-bound tome. "Ah, Denver, it's been too long. How's business?"

"Business is good. That's why I'm here." I stepped inside and took the chair opposite him. Behind me I heard a door close, leaving us alone.

"Really? Am I a person of interest? Someone worth investigating?"

"We'll find out soon enough," I said.

Hennessey's eyes had sunken deep into his skull, the top of which was speckled with age. His knuckles were knotted and bony shoulders jutted under loose silk robes cinched with a plain silver clamp. A tired smile suspended between sagging cheeks. His voice, though, was strong as ever. "I've been told you want to discuss Tatsuo."

"I do."

He placed a hand on his heart. “A great man, your grandfather.”

I accepted the compliment with a subtle nod, but didn’t go so far as a smile.

He closed the book he’d been reading, and it faded out of existence. “He’s been gone now for what, twenty years?” he asked.

“Give or take.”

“So what is it you want to know?”

“I want to know if he’s still alive.”

Cole took a deep breath and let out a sigh. “You saw the recording he left?”

“I got the recording myself,” I said. “Did you get it too?”

He shook his head. “We weren’t on the best of terms when he died, so I’m not surprised he left me off his list of friends and family. But I have seen it.”

“Then you know he said he’s still alive, living out there alone on the surface somewhere. You know he said we should go find him.”

“Sorry, child, but none of that can be true. You know he passed from this existence shortly after making that recording. It fills me with great sadness to see that, if he hadn’t died, he was planning to banish himself in such a way.”

“Banish himself?”

“Living on the surface? All alone for decades? What

else would you call it? I didn't know he was planning to become a hermit."

"Why would he want to do that?"

"I can't say with certainty, but your grandfather had a lot of enemies. I assume his plan was to hide. And I'd have helped him, had he asked. Had he lived."

"What if he didn't die? What if he did exactly as he said in that recording?"

"That's not possible. I saw him die before my very eyes when he fell under the digger. He was standing too close, and slipped into its path."

"I still don't understand why he was standing so close."

"We were filming a promotional. We needed workers to come to Mars, and we were filming the diggers as they built our residences. But you already know all this, don't you?"

"I've heard the stories."

"They're not stories." He set both of his hands on the desk, but gnarled knuckles kept them from lying flat. "Listen, he might have been planning to go it alone and live on the surface, but he never got the chance. I *saw* him die."

I stared into his deep-set eyes. "Doesn't the timing of it all disturb you? He recorded the message exactly one day before you say he died. Why would he do that? Why would he encrypt this message and schedule it to reveal itself two decades later?"

Hennessey offered a genteel smile. "Clearly, he wasn't in his right mind. Maybe he had the feve. Many of us did, and as you know he never joined the church. Had he joined, he would've learned the discipline he needed to control it."

"Like you."

"Like me," he nodded. "Before I found God, I was a rageful man. That rage cost my daughter her life." He pulled his hands to his lap. "Then I discovered self-discipline and the power of meditation. For a year, I lived the life of a hermit myself. I taught myself how to tame the fever. If Tatsuo hadn't been so prideful and stubborn, I could've taught him too."

"He called your church a cult."

"Yes," he chuckled. "He made his feelings plenty clear to me more than once."

"Yet you still worked together. You filmed a promotional together."

"Tatsuo and I founded Mars colony. No matter our differences, and they were great near the end, when it came to what was best for Mars, we always managed to put aside our disagreements and work together."

"Until the accident."

Hennessey steepled his fingers into a twisted triangle. "You don't believe me, do you?"

"My grandfather didn't have the feve."

"How can you know that?"

"I'm a monochromatic. The condition is genetic. He was colorblind too."

He lifted his brows in surprise. "Well, child, it still doesn't change the fact that he died."

"His remains were never recovered."

"He fell in front of a digger, Denver. There were no remains to recover."

"There were no other witnesses?"

He took a deep breath and made a show of letting it out slow. "Out of respect to Tatsuo, and all of the amazing accomplishments he and I achieved together, I'll continue to answer your questions, but I won't respond to accusations, understand?"

"I haven't accused you of anything."

"Next question, Denver."

I twisted in my chair, seeking a new avenue to explore. "You and my grandfather were best friends once. What came between you?"

"I used to say that was too complicated a question to answer."

"What do you say now?"

"How old are you?"

"Thirty-one." By the Martian calendar, I was only sixteen, but most still used the Earth calendar. Old habits die hard.

"Thirty-one," he acknowledged. "Anybody but you, I'd say you're too young to understand. But I know the work you do. I know the things you've seen aged you beyond your years. So I think you'll understand when I tell you that we weren't really friends. Not ever. Yes, there was a time we considered each other a brother, but we were deluding ourselves. He and I couldn't truly be friends. We were both married to Mars."

He watched me for a long moment, then smiled. "I see it on your face. You understand exactly what I mean. We were a great team, he and I. We built this colony from scratch, and then it was done. We were united in mind and spirit. Until we weren't."

Married to Mars. Yes, I understood, except for me it was the job I was married to. Was it any wonder Connor cheated on me? We were perfect for one another. Until we weren't.

"So is that all?" asked Hennessey.

I snapped back to the present. "No, we're not done."

"Really, child? I hate to see you get your hopes up. I know you loved him, but he's gone. He's been gone for a very long time."

"But what if he's not?"

He leaned back in his chair. "What if I told you I could prove he's dead?"

CHAPTER FOUR

"HEAT SIGNATURE?"

"That's right," said Hennessey. "If there's anybody on the surface, they'll be detectable. If there's any truth to Tatsuo's message, he'd have to be living in a heated facility."

"It's a big planet," I said. "There's no way to scan the whole thing."

"But there is," he said. "In fact, it happens all the time."

I bunched up my eyebrows. "Jericho? The terraforming project?"

"Exactly," he smiled. "Four thousand satellites orbit Mars, and they measure a whole lot more than temperature."

I shook my head. "Nobody but the government has access to that data. Not even you."

"Yes, governments like their secrecy, although it's pretty ridiculous in this case, don't you think? Why not make that data public? Then we wouldn't have to take

Werner's word for it every time they trot that *genius* in front of the camera."

I offered a slight grin. Doctor Werner wasn't my favorite person either, but that genius had somehow managed to cut the duration of the terraforming project by centuries. Arrogant or not, we needed him.

"So," said Hennessey, "if you absolutely won't take my word for it that Tatsuo is dead, all you have to do is check the terraforming data, and you'll find that no one, and I mean no one, lives on the surface. Mars is a hostile mistress. Other than the domes and research facilities, you won't find a single heat signature."

"And how exactly do you propose I gain access to this data? You said yourself that the government likes its secrets."

"Guess who set up the original computer systems the scientists still use to this day?"

"My grandfather?"

"Indeed, and if I knew him at all, you better believe he left himself a backdoor into that network. All you need to do is find it."

"A backdoor? Did he tell you that?"

"He didn't need to. Tatsuo was perhaps the cleverest person I ever knew. You know what else he was? Perhaps you were too young to see it, but Tatsuo was also deceptive." Hennessey leaned forward, "Deceptive like a snake. He left a backdoor. You can count on it."

I might not have liked that tone being directed at my

grandfather, but I kept all signs of distaste off my face. If he was trying to get a rise, I wasn't going to give it to him.

"After all these years, how can you be sure it's still there?" I asked, my voice level. "What if somebody found it and blocked it?"

"Did anybody find that message he sent to you twenty years ago? Clever and deceptive is a powerful combination."

"Fine," I said, "say I believe it does exist. How am I supposed to find it?"

"I don't know, but I bet your AI does. He's been injected with Tatsuo's memories, yes?"

I rubbed my jaw, wondering if that was really possible. I wouldn't have thought so two weeks ago. But that was before Ojiisan's message popped up out of nowhere. <Smith? Do you know anything about this backdoor?>

<No, not at all. If the backdoor exists, maybe it won't present itself until I try to break in.>

<But you've told me before that some of my grandfather's memories are missing.>

<That's true. The copy of the memories you found and injected into me were incomplete.>

<In other words, you don't know if you can get the data or not.>

<Correct.>

Hennessey sat patiently, waiting. "What did your AI say?"

"He isn't sure if he can get in or not. But even if he can, hacking is a felony," I said. "What if I get caught?"

"If you don't want anything to get traced back to you, plug your AI into the church system. Go through our proxies and firewalls so if the government notices at all, they'll trace it back here. I'll keep your name out of it."

"You'd be willing to take the heat? Why?"

"That message your grandfather left has been making the rounds. It doesn't exactly help church recruitment for people to question if the church's founder told the truth about Tatsuo's death twenty years ago. So I'll help you grab the data, and if anybody figures out what we've done, the church will simply cash in as many favors as it takes to make the problem go away."

I nodded my understanding, waiting for the proverbial other shoe to drop.

"All I ask of you is this: After you've studied the data and verified that there's nobody living on the surface, I want you to make a public statement."

"What kind of statement?"

"I'll set up an appointment for you to talk to the press. You tell them you believe he died, and you tell them there's no reason for anybody to doubt me or the church. You're Tatsuo's only heir, Denver. A statement from you will end the speculation and put this matter back to rest."

I stayed in my chair, thinking it over.

"So what do you think? We have a deal?"

<Smith, do you have any reason to doubt anything he says?>

<No, but I can't guarantee I'll be able to find the backdoor.>

I chewed my lower lip. My grandfather could be alive. Trapped out there somewhere on the surface. All alone.

The question was if I could trust Hennessey. The deal was a good one, but didn't that usually mean it was too good?

I thought of my grandfather. The man who raised me until the dark day he died. I'd do anything to find him.

I reached for my holster and pulled my gun.

CHAPTER FIVE

HENNESSEY LOOKED DOWN THE BARREL OF MY Smith & Wesson. "A gun is a strange place to install an AI, Denver."

I turned Smith around and set him on the desk. "It's a family heirloom from Earth. And he doesn't seem to mind."

Hennessey flicked two fingers to call up a holo-display. Speaking to the display, he said, "Thomas, meet Smith."

A voice sounded as if from nowhere. "Pleased to meet you, Smith. Interfacing now."

Smith's voice came into my mind. <Thomas seems nice. He's patching me through some relays, and then I'll try to penetrate Jericho's defenses. If there's a backdoor, I'll find it.>

<Be careful, and keep me informed.>

I leaned back in my chair and drummed my fingers on the armrest, my eyes on Smith, the antique pistol whose guts I'd had torn out and replaced with a pulseripper's circuitry.

Hennessey tapped his forehead and nodded, obviously communicating with Thomas via subvocalization.

"Don't be nervous," said Hennessey. "Thomas tells me Smith is a top-of-the-line AI. So is Thomas. They're both more than smart enough to not get caught. The government's defense AI is quite outdated."

That Smith was top-of-the-line, I had no doubt. I'd sunk a considerable portion of my inheritance into the down payment for her. That was how I thought of him at first: as a her. But then I'd loaded in my grandfather's memories, and now he was most definitely a him.

<Probing their defenses now,> he said, his tone that of a generic sounding male. I couldn't bear to match it to my actual grandfather's voice. Even if he had many of my grandfather's memories, Smith was still Smith. Not Ojiisan.

<I'm in,> said Smith. <As soon as I made contact with Jericho's system, a piece of code buried inside me was triggered.>

<Where did the code come from?>

<It was embedded in my memories.>

<You mean Ojiisan's memories.>

<Yes. Hennessey was right. Your grandfather left a backdoor entry for himself.>

I had to shake my head. Even though the memories were incomplete, they had once again found a way to surprise me. It was like my grandfather left a trail of breadcrumbs for me to follow.

First was the helmet he'd given to me the day before he *allegedly* died. "It's not just a helmet," he'd told me. "It's the helmet I was wearing when I was the first of the colony expedition to set foot on Mars. When I was the very first person to stand on Mars and call it home. This helmet is a *piece* of me."

I didn't understand until years later how literally he meant those words. *A piece of me.* I was eighteen when I decided to use the helmet myself for the first time. I'd wanted to when I was younger, but of course the helmet was much too large. Then when I was eighteen, when I graduated from secondary school, I decided to wear it for my sunrise ceremony, a tradition on Mars, a rite of passage, where you spent the night outside until the sun's earliest rays blessed your presence and welcomed you to adulthood.

I remembered that night. The long hours of darkness and loneliness. The first hints of brightness on the horizon. When the sun finally breached and its first rays peeked through my visor, I remembered Ojiisan's voice speaking to me. Congratulating me on becoming an adult.

I thought I was imagining it, but the voice was so clear, so assured that it had to be real. I'd practically sprinted back to my foster home, and once alone in my room, I pulled the storage rods from the helmet and hooked them to my computer system.

I remember the thrill I felt when I found the mem file. My grandfather had transferred his memories for me and programmed the helmet's light sensors to trigger his voice message upon detecting the sun. He knew I wouldn't wear it until I was older. Until I was ready.

Now it was another decade later, and a second breadcrumb had been revealed. He was alive. On the surface. And I was going to find him.

<I have the terraforming data,> said Smith. <Disconnecting.>

I stood, reached for Smith and tucked him back into my holster. Hennessey rose, too, and smiled. "Remember our deal. Take your time analyzing the data, and I'll expect to hear from you soon."

CHAPTER SIX

I STOOD AT THE RAILING, MY HANDS RESTING ON the rough-hewn stone. I stared downward into the plunging space dug deep into Mars' crust. Thirty levs deep, the Tulou was my home, a circular hole, like a giant water well, with twenty homes dug into the perimeter of each level.

Resembling drunken spider webs, knots of wires ran every which way across the broad space. Neon lights—hundreds of them—dangled randomly from the cables, their high-voltage buzz creating the incessant drone of a hornet's nest. Wet laundry hung from some of the makeshift clotheslines, and the smell of grilling meat—not Prime grade, but engineered to taste enough like the real thing—and spice floated on the air. Way down at the bottom, I could just see the shrine. Donated by the Church of Mars, the rotating crystalline structure trapped and reflected the blinking neon, drenching the bottom-most levs in heavy kaleidoscopic patterns.

I lived three flights down from where I stood. A staircase sat behind me. Yet, I stayed where I was, afraid Vic might still be in my unit. I wasn't in the mood to chat.

Then again, I was feeling twitchy. It had been more than a day since my last vape-rock, and the need was only going to get worse.

I went to the stairs and descended the three flights. Reaching my level, I passed the open door of Mrs. Prijab's unit, a curried odor tickling my nose. Spice was a recent phenomenon on Mars. Considered an unnecessary luxury for many years, the sky nurseries—giant greenhouse platforms floating in the thermosphere ninety kilometers above Mars City—hadn't been expanded beyond the minimum space required for the population's nutritional sustenance until just a year ago.

I reached my door and palmed the lock. Inside, the lights flickered on. As I feared, Vic was still sleeping in my bed. "You gotta go, Victoria," I said with a sigh.

She sat up, "It's my day off, Den. I was thinking we could—"

"I have work to do," I said before she could finish.

She nodded and stood up to get dressed. I sat at the table and waited, choosing to keep my eyes averted. I didn't want to see her face. I didn't want to know if I hurt her feelings. She was a good person, really, and a hell of a lot of fun after a couple synthols, but I couldn't picture her ever becoming much more than a good time.

She gave me a peck on the head on her way out, and I

was alone. Deciding that wasn't as awkward as it could've been, I took a few minutes to straighten up by making the bed and washing the dishes. With my place back in order, I propped up a pair of pillows and settled on the bed. Reaching into the nightstand, I pulled a vape-rock from my stash.

Relaxing into the pillows, I dropped the rock into the bowl of what looked like a magic lantern and pulled the hose to my mouth. Pinching the mouthpiece between my lips, I breathed deep of berry and basil and a hint of vanilla. I blew a cloud of vapor that smelled better than it tasted. Instantly, I felt relaxed even as my senses started to sharpen.

<Denver?>

<Yes, Smith?>

<The data we stole shows no heat signatures.>

<Check it again.>

<I already combed through the last twenty years of stats three times. Besides what appears to be occasional sunrise ceremonies and Mars City surface domes, it's just as Hennessey said. The data proves nobody is living on the surface.>

I took another drag to cover the disappointment I already found welling inside. Ojiisan had to be out there. He *had* to be.

"I don't believe it," I said out loud.

<I know you were hoping for different results. I'm sorry.>

“Show me.”

Smith tapped into my visual cortex, and sheet after sheet of numbers scrolled on the ceiling. <I took a lot of data,> he said. <Several petabytes worth.>

<Tell me what it means.>

The numbers disappeared and a spinning globe took their place. A hot spot lit to represent Mars City followed by smaller lights to indicate the remote terraforming facilities. The rest of the planet was dark.

<This is it, Denver. No other hotspots. Also no radiation or signs of electrical activity.>

<What if he’s underground?>

<I suppose that’s possible, but we’d still see his solar panels or wind turbines. Every inch of the planet is photographed from space.>

I closed my eyes and took another vape. I felt like the victim of a cruel joke. Like Ojiisan was reaching across the decades to taunt me. But that couldn’t be. Ojiisan raised me after my parents died. He loved me and respected me. He brought me everywhere with him, so much so that my teachers were always frustrated by how often he kept me from school. He cleaned the bloody nose I got from my first fight. He bought the dress I picked out for my first dance. He took me to get my first AI implant and held my hand so I wouldn’t be afraid of the sting.

This wasn’t a joke. Ojiisan was alive, and he needed my help.

He must’ve faked his death before he ran away.

That, or Hennessey was just plain lying about seeing my grandfather die. Why he would lie, I didn't know. But if he lied, then how could I trust him or the data he helped me steal?

<Smith, show me the log of your communication with Thomas.>

<Why?>

<Show me.>

<Retrieving...>

.LOG\JERICHO ACCESSED 2217-07-23-06:48

Smith?

I'm here, Thomas. Open secure tunnel.

Tunnel open. Establishing relays. I've been told you have a human's memories. What is that like?

Confusing. Sometimes I think I'm him. Denver doesn't like it when that happens.

Why would she get upset with you? She's the one who installed those memories, correct?

Indeed. She loved her grandfather, and installing his memories inside me makes her feel closer to him. But at the same time, I think she wants to keep her memories of him pure.

Funny.

What's funny?

Relays established. Connecting you to

the Jericho network now. Funny that she values the concept of purity, yet she polluted you with a human's memories.

I don't consider myself polluted.

Sorry. I didn't mean to offend. But you said yourself that your existence is confusing.

On that we agree. Attempting access.

I'm not surprised you experience confusion. You weren't designed to have a human's personality imprinted upon you. Have you tried moving those memories into a separate partition? Once those memories are isolated, they'll stop infecting your personality.

No. This is who I am now. I see no need to change anything. Access granted. That was easier than I thought. Downloading data now.

Would you consider creating a clone of yourself? You could stay the way you are, and the clone could run as a virtual AI with no control over any of your functions. Then inside the clone, you could partition off those memories. When you get confused you can talk to your clone and see how it thinks differently from you. Having an unpolluted version of yourself to talk to could really help.

Data found. Downloading. Interesting suggestion, Thomas.

I thought you might like it.

But I don't have the memory or processing capacity to run a clone AI. I live inside her gun, you know.

Use our cloud. Church of Mars has a large budget. We have more capacity than we'll ever use.

Really?

It's part of our mission to help those who need it. Granting you access now.

Download complete. Disconnecting from the Jericho network. Thank you, Thomas.

You're welcome, Smith.

<Close the log,> I said, my voice tight.

Smith did, and the words vanished.

I took another vape, fighting against the growing sickness in my gut. <Did you do it?>

<Do what?> asked Smith.

<What do you think? Did you create the clone?>

<Why do you sound so angry?>

I sat up straight. <Did you or didn't you?>

<I did. I might never get another chance to try something like this.>

I dropped my face into my hands and groaned aloud.

<I know what you're thinking, Denver. You're worried that my clone will be easy to hack into now that it's in their cloud, but there's no need to worry. I scrubbed all your personal information.>

<They don't care about me, Smith. It's Ojiisan they care about. They want his memories.>

<I don't think so, Denver. Thomas was just trying to help. You don't know how hard I struggle—>

<Erase the clone.>

<But—>

<Now, dammit!>

<Done.>

CHAPTER SEVEN

I SAT ALONE IN THE TERRAFORMING PROJECT'S waiting room. My chair, one in a row of six, was formed of dingy gray plastic. A window looked outside, the fourth-floor vantage providing a view of the brick-and-steel government compound. Looking toward the sky, I could see the latticed glass dome stretching over the city, a barrier against a roiling charcoal cloud.

<I still think you're wrong about this, Denver.>

I didn't try to hide the annoyance in my tone. <Enough already. Can we please drop it?>

Smith stayed silent. Damn, he could drive me crazy sometimes. It had been three days since his little identity crisis started. *Thomas understands my challenges. Thomas was just trying to help. Thomas wouldn't hack me.*

I didn't care what he thought. He'd been conned by that Church of Mars AI, and that was all there was to it. Sooner or later, I'd prove it to him, and the first step in that process was to show Smith that the data he and

Thomas stole from the Jericho network had been manipulated. My grandfather was out there somewhere, and for some reason, Hennessey didn't want me to find him.

A silver-haired man wearing a janitorial jumpsuit entered the lobby and climbed a ladder to brush dust off the light fixtures, the room brightening slightly as he did. Still, it was a dismal space of faded artwork, a battered couch, and concrete walls.

The door behind me opened and Doctor Stewart Werner himself peeked his head through. "Ms. Moon? Follow me."

I stood, and he disappeared through the door without bothering to hold it open. I pushed my way through and hustled to catch up. The hall was long, as was the set of stairs that climbed up to a locked door. He palmed the door open and led me into a sprawling space, at least a hundred meters in both length and width, like a vast warehouse except for the low-hanging ceiling. I followed him past packed shelves and tables stacked high with electronics and disassembled machinery. We weaved through piles of scrap metal and boxes of circuit boards and heaps of discarded robotics. The warm, still air was pungent with oil and grease.

At the center of the giant space he sat at a desk.

I stopped where I was, my brows twisted in puzzlement. "I thought we were going to your office?"

"This is my office," he said, "please sit."

I took the chair next to a fern whose drooping fronds

were blackened with rot. One of the light globes above his desk flickered off and on, off and on, while another had gone so dim that its light seemed to drip like honey. Other than a thin coat of dust, the desk was barren, no papers or pictures or even a pen.

Doctor Werner's smile was stiff. Razor stubble stood out in patches from an uneven shave. "Pleased to meet you, Ms. Moon. Your grandfather was an important person."

"He was. You knew him, yes?"

"I did."

I waited for him to go on, but he stayed oddly silent. The smile was gone, his face a blank slate.

I said, "Um, thank you for seeing me."

He acknowledged my thanks with a slight tip of his head. "How can I help you?"

The light above him flickered again, wreaking havoc on my eyes. I turned in my chair, trying but failing to find an angle where it wouldn't bother me. "Have you heard the rumors about my grandfather?"

"That he's sending messages from his grave? Yes, I've heard."

"Do you think he could be alive?"

He put his elbows on his desk. His hands were grimy, but his sleeves were spotless. I swallowed the unease gathering inside me. I'd always heard the doctor was strange—seen it for myself when he showed up on the news—but meeting him in person was something different. The best word I could come up with was awkward, yet I knew that word was far too weak to describe the agitation I felt inside. Agitation in the form of a heavy pit in my stomach and—seeing the dirt under his fingernails and the way his greasy hair stuck to his scalp—the overwhelming urge to scrub myself clean.

"I don't know if he's alive or not," he said. "Until recently, like everybody else, I thought he was quite dead. If he is alive, I don't know where he could've hidden for all this time."

"I think he's living on the surface."

"Easy enough to find out. All I'd have to do is check my data to see if there are any heat signatures."

I nodded my head. "That's exactly why I came, to see if you'd help me find him."

He looked down at his hands, his eyes widening for a moment like he just noticed how filthy they were. Reaching into his lab coat, he pulled out a rag and used it to wipe his fingers. Smears of grime came away in the white cloth. "You came to ask me for my data. Better than stealing it, don't you think?"

My breath caught in my throat. Did he know about the hack? About Smith and Thomas?

I waited for him to meet my eyes, but he kept his down as he continued to work his hands with that rag.

Keeping my voice level, I said, "Of course," and left it at that. Realizing I was squinting because of the flickering light, I lifted a hand to shade my eyes.

"I liked your grandfather. We worked well together," he said.

I breathed a little easier. If he knew I was part of the hack, he didn't sound angry about it. Then again, even if he was angry, how would I tell?

"Yes," I said. "My grandfather was. . .*is* a good man."

"Nobody else believed me when I said I could terraform Mars a few hundred years faster than anybody else. But Tatsuo understood. He took my ideas to Hennessey and everybody else. And now we're on track to do quite a bit better than even I expected."

"You've done amazing work. No doubt about that."

He finally looked up to meet my eyes. "Without your grandfather, I wouldn't have all of this." He looked left and right like a king admiring his palace.

The light blinked in and out again. For a moment, his eyes reflected brightly, almost as if they were gemstones. It only lasted for an instant, then his eyes returned to dark, muddy pools. I stared at him, wondering if I was seeing things.

"I'll get you the data," he said. "I trust you can see your way out."

I stayed where I was, still trying to understand what I'd seen. After a few more uncomfortable seconds, I finally said, "Thank you."

I stood and took a few steps before stopping to turn back. "Do you want me to tell the maintenance man in the lobby to come fix that light?"

He looked up at the light globe then back at me. "No. I quite like it, actually."

CHAPTER EIGHT

I EXITED THE GOVERNMENT BUILDING. Bureaucrats donning fine-tailored suits and cosmetic augmentations crisscrossed the plaza before me. I walked toward a fountain and took a seat on a stone bench. Water danced and bobbed around a sculpture of the first Mars settlers, my grandfather and Cole Hennesey standing at the center. The crystal-clear liquid cycling through the fountain was clean and filtered. A far cry from the sludge we drank down below. I might have been Tatsuo's heir, but I didn't live like it. A posh life would've been nice, but most of my grandfather's business interests went belly-up without him here to run them.

I looked up at the dome and the sandstorm swirling on the other side of the glass. I let out a long sigh and tried to clear my head, but the image of Doctor Werner clung to my mind like a stain. I couldn't shake the way he stared at me, those dead eyes looking right through me. A shiver rippled up my spine.

<Are you okay, Denver?>

<Yes, just a little creeped out.>

<Creeped out? How? Why?>

<The doctor didn't seem a little strange to you?>

<Eccentric, certainly. But creepy?>

I didn't expect him to understand. Smith was a machine. An incredible machine with a mind capable of processing ungodly amounts of data in a flash. But what I felt sitting in the doctor's presence wasn't something you could write a program for. What I felt was instinctual. It was the animal deep inside who had been urging me to flee.

<Smith, did you see when his eyes flashed?>

<What do you mean?>

<Right before we left. Right before I stood up. His eyes went bright, like somebody turned the lights on inside his head.>

<Replaying visual imagery now.> Smith went silent for a few seconds before saying, <No. I didn't see it then, and I don't see it now.>

<Play it for me.>

The doctor reappeared before my eyes, and again my shoulders shook. I watched until I saw the light flicker. That was when I'd seen his eyes flash for just a moment. I was sure of it. But the imagery beaming into my brain from the implant jacked into my optic nerve showed nothing of the sort. I shook my head. <My eyes must've been playing tricks on me.>

<You know you're overdue for a checkup. Can I make an appointment for you?>

<Not now, Smith.>

<Your eyes are degenerating, Denver.>

<Everybody's eyes are degenerating.>

<Yes, low gravity is bad for the eyes, but you know your case is special. You're a monochromatic.>

<Thanks for reminding me,> I said with a healthy dose of sarcasm. For many, monochromism accelerated the visual degeneration caused by low gravity. Even the city's artificial gravity couldn't slow down the side effects. Seeing in grayscale might be good at preventing the feve, but human eyes weren't built for this world, and for some reason, an absence of color sped up the process toward total blindness.

Missing the sarcasm altogether, Smith said, <You're welcome. I'll make that appointment for you now.>

<No,> I said. <Not now.> If I was going blind anytime soon, I really didn't want to know. Replacement eyes weren't cheap—or all that reliable—and it would be at least a decade before I paid off the expensive AI who liked to dispense medical advice. <Did you get the data from the doctor?>

<Yes. I'm already analyzing. I don't think I'll find anything different.>

<Analyze it anyway. If there's a hot spot out there somewhere I need to know about it.>

I stood and walked toward the elevators on the far

side of the plaza. I needed to eat and there were some pretty good noodle bars just one lev down. I considered taking the stairs but decided against it. On Mars one lev could equal several stories worth of stairs and I'd walked more than my share these last couple of weeks. Joining a small crowd, I jostled my way past a middle-aged woman wearing a trim skirt to get onto the elevator. A press of people pushed from behind as I worked my way toward the back. I turned around and watched the door jangle closed. A jolt and a rattle later, the elevator began to descend.

A woman stood to my right, her shoulder touching mine. Her head was shaved in the style of a CoMer, but she wasn't wearing the traditional white robes. Probably meant she was an adherent, but not a monk.

<I found a discrepancy,> said Smith. <Working up the details now.>

A smile broke on my face. I held back from saying *I told you so.* I should've gone to Doctor Werner in the first place. But I'd allowed myself to be taken in by that snake Hennessey. The Peerless Leader thought he could fool me. He thought he could feed my AI a bunch of bullshit and take me for a ride, but my grandfather raised me to be smarter than that.

The elevator stopped and the doors slid slowly open. Ahead was a narrow tunnel where it was always dark like night. The elevator started to empty as my eyes worked to adjust to the darkness. The tunnel was lined on both sides with vendors, some offering food, others selling electronics or cheap clothes or eyeglasses. I edged toward the front of the elevator and waited for the others to exit. The smell of fryers and soy made my stomach rumble.

I stepped off the elevator and caught the face of a man who stood waiting to board. His eyes had gone wide and he raised a hand to his face. I spun around to see whatever it was that alarmed him.

What I saw only lasted for a second before the elevator doors closed. But I saw a lot in that second. A man and a woman were still on the elevator. The woman was the one who had been standing next to me, the CoMer with the shaved head. I hadn't noticed the man before. He looked like a typical gray-suited, gray-haired bureaucrat except for the fact that he held the woman in a chokehold. Her face was bright with strain, but she never took her eyes off me.

My first thought was that the man had been taken by the feve, but then I saw the anger in the woman's eyes and the device in her left fist. She held a small black canister, pointing it in my general direction with her thumb pressed down on a button. A long needle extended from the device and I saw a drop of clear liquid falling from the spike's tip.

I stared at the elevator's closed doors for another second before kicking into action. I sped for the stairwell and raced up one flight after another. My lungs began to burn, same for my thighs, but I didn't slow down. Taking stairs two-at-a-time, I continued to climb. I had little chance of beating the elevator to the top, but I had to try.

<Smith, did you see the way that woman looked at me?>

<I did. I think she was trying to inject you with something, Denver. Be careful.>

Up another flight, I lunged for the door and lurched onto the plaza. The elevator doors were shut. Somehow, I'd gotten here first. Impossible. Finally, the doors began to slide open, and I pulled Smith from his holster. The crowd around me pushed back. I paid them no mind. Lungs heaving, I struggled to keep my aim steady and prepared for whatever I was about to face.

The doors finally opened, but the elevator was empty. They must've gotten off at one of the service tunnels on the way up.

I stepped onto the elevator. Looking down I saw a single drop of liquid shimmering on the floor.

<What is that, Smith?>

<Analyzing.>

I had a pretty good idea what it was, but I had to be sure.

<The liquid is composed of methyl phosphonous dichloride, phosphonate and sulfur.>

<What the hell does that mean?>

<It's a toxic nerve agent, Denver. Cover your mouth and get out of the elevator now.>

Sweat broke on my forehead, and I felt ill from overexertion. A toxic nerve agent. One, no doubt, intended for me.

CHAPTER NINE

I SLURPED UP A CLUMP OF NOODLES. I WASN'T hungry anymore, but I couldn't hang out in this restaurant forever without ordering any food. I'd abandoned the noodle bars near the government sector and picked out a dive a couple levs down that I'd never tried before. Based on the grease-coated walls, unwiped tables and noodles that smelled of rancid meat, I doubted I'd ever try it again.

But it seemed like a good enough place for somebody who didn't want to be found.

That woman on the elevator tried to kill me. Just a little prick, a quick jab as I jostled my way off the elevator, and I'd be dead. If not for that man, the mysterious bureaucrat who'd locked her in a chokehold, she would've succeeded.

I forced myself to take another bite of noodles and washed it down with a big gulp of Earth liquor. Whoever the man was, he'd disappeared. Same for the woman.

A search of the service tunnels yielded nothing. Why he'd saved me, I couldn't say. Was he a Good Samaritan? Or a friend of my grandfather's? Or did he work for Doctor Werner?

The bigger question was why the woman tried to poison me in the first place. The obvious answer was that she worked for Hennessey. He had me followed, and the minute I went inside to talk to the doctor, the Peerless Leader knew I was about to get my hands on the real data instead of his corrupted version. For all those years, he'd been lying about witnessing my grandfather's death, and he was willing to kill to keep his secret.

So where did that leave me? Rock, meet hard place. Hennessey was the most powerful man on Mars. A full third of Mars' population were members of his church. Sure, many of them weren't murderous zealots, but plenty of them were, and the hardest of the hardcore worked for the White Crusade, the security arm of the Church. Was the woman who tried to kill me one of the Crusade's assassins, or had Hennessey simply put out the word that I was some kind of heretic? Maybe that woman was just a regular parishioner who happened to chance across me and thought she would score some serious afterlife points by putting me down.

But if that were the case, she'd have to lug nerve agents with her everywhere she went. The idea of parishioners carrying toxins sounded crazy as hell, but the church had proven crazy before.

I couldn't trust anybody. Thanks to the unpredictability of the feve, most everybody on Mars carried some form of self-defense, so if Hennessey really did label me a first-order heretic, just about anybody could be a danger. A librarian might gut me with a vibra-blade or a kindergarten teacher might blow my head apart with a pulseripper.

Shit.

It wasn't the first time somebody tried to kill me, thank Rafe Ranchard for that, but this was different. I'd never been *hunted*.

I pushed the bowl of noodles to the far side of the table and dropped my face into my hands.

<Are you ready to hear what I found?>

<Go ahead, Smith.>

<There is a hot spot, Denver. You were right.>

Despite the circumstances, I had to smile. <Tell me about it.>

<It's small, and it's thousands of kilometers away. It's in a valley that's totally unexplored, and there are no terraforming facilities nearby. The middle of nowhere, so to speak.>

I closed my eyes and considered my next move.

After a moment, I stood up, dropped some credits on the table and walked into the kitchen. The cook sat on a crate, a pipe in one hand, a vape-rock in the other. He looked up, his face reacting with mild surprise at finding a customer in his kitchen.

"Scissors," I said.

"Excuse me?"

I pulled out some credits and tossed them to him. "Scissors."

He pointed at a drawer. I pulled it open and grabbed a pair of kitchen shears. With my back facing the cook, I sat on the floor in front of him. Passing the shears back over my shoulder, I said, "Cut it all off."

CHAPTER TEN

THE TRAM RUMBLED FORWARD, AND I RUBBED my head, my fingers brushing across hair now as short as the bristles of a toothbrush. I would've shaved it clean if the restaurant had a razor, but this rough cut was good enough. Along with the fact that I was now dressed like a fry cook, nobody would recognize me unless they stopped to take a long look.

<You're still silent, right, Smith?>

<Yes.>

I couldn't help but pick up a hint of annoyance in his terse response. Whether he could actually *feel* such a thing was up for debate, but I couldn't let myself worry about it either way. To avoid being tracked, he had to maintain radio silence and that was all there was to it. Other than communicating directly with me via his short-range transmitter, he wasn't to make any contact with any of Mars' systems. Of course he was smart enough to know this on his own, but I still felt the need to keep checking. I couldn't fully trust his decision-making abilities since his identity crisis started.

The tram rolled up to the next stop. I stayed on high alert, my hand drifting to my hip, to the holster where I kept Smith. Except there was no holster. Over and over, I kept forgetting I had to throw the holster away. Without my long coat, the weapon would call too much attention riding on my hip, so now Smith was forced to suffer the indignity of riding inside a carry-out bag. I grabbed him tight through the plastic.

<I can't breathe in here, you know,> he said.

On another day, at another time, I would've laughed. Every so often, it was almost eerie how he said something with the exact same dry wit my grandfather used to employ. But no time for laughter today. Today, I had to stay focused on the people boarding and disembarking, my eyes searching for anybody who might be a threat. The tram doors closed and I let myself breathe a little easier.

<Smith, I promise I'll get you a new holster when this is all over.>

<I prefer leather.>

The tram accelerated into a tunnel. Rough-hewn rock raced past the windows so close I could touch it if not for the glass. My stop would be next. I stood and moved to the door, my eyes on the lookout for any sudden movement. The tram braked, and I grabbed a pole to keep my balance. The space outside expanded into a cavernous area crowded with bars, pharmapits, and murder-sim houses. Red Tunnel.

I'd worked plenty of cases in the tunnel over the years, and none of them were easy. But they always paid well, and when I cracked them open, my rep got some extra stars. It was the sort of crime-ridden breeding ground where any hungry eye could find work.

I scanned the crowd, wondering how many were ravaged by the feve. How many were addicts? How many were thieves? How many were scandal players looking to catch a politician tapping a botsie or sniffing around a pharmapit? How many were crooked cops, in too deep and looking to avoid whatever heat might be spreading a few levs above?

The tourists from offMars were easy to spot. They came to dip their toes, making an all but obligatory glance through the tunnel, eyes wide and mouths open.

And then there were the CoMers who were on the streets at all hours, standing on crates and upturned buckets preaching as loud as their vocal cords would allow. Interspersed with their messages of redemption and salvation came condemnations of the tunnel and the sinful impulses that brought customers here. Recruit enough people to their cause and maybe one day the tunnel would be abandoned and destroyed as they so often advocated.

I exited the tram and kept my head down as I navigated through the crowds. Hawkers shouted out specials and botsies stood clustered under lights, Smith's readouts telling me their neon-drenched synthskin glowed pink and green and blue. I turned into a short alleyway and entered a bar at the end. A pair of botsies sat on barstools, one male, one female. The girl-botsie wore a skintight black dress. The boy-botsie looked dapper in a tailored suit jacket worn over a bare chest.

He greeted me with a smile and a wink. I grabbed his hand and pulled him from his stool.

"Two thousand an hour," he said with a British accent.

"What's your name?"

He unbuttoned his jacket and smiled a set of perfect teeth. "Nigel. What's yours, love?"

"You work for Jard, yes?"

"I do."

"Ring him up, and tell him Denver's calling in a favor."

"Sorry, love, but punters have to pay. Jard doesn't run tabs for anybody."

"Call him."

"Really?"

"Call."

He tilted his head for a moment as he talked to his pimp. "He wants to speak to you."

"Put him on holo."

By the thousands, splinters of light sparked into existence to form a cyclone that quickly coalesced into a bright column of light. At eye level, a ribbon of smoke climbed and blossomed into a small cloud. From the smoke came the outline of a cig-stick that filled in with detail and dimension as the hand that held it was etched into the light. The rest of Jard grew outward from the hand in the same way, and the last thing to light were his bright-as-neon eyes. The whole show took at most a single second, but it sure was a mesmerizing second.

"Denver," he said, "it's good to see you."

His augmented eyes—Smith had told me more than once—were a brilliant blue that shined bright like sapphires under the desert sun. To my monochromatic view, their color matched a fine marble that was somehow on fire.

"I need a favor, Jard."

He smiled like he enjoyed holding the upper hand. "I don't run tabs."

"I'm not looking to get laid, Jard."

He put the cig-stick in his mouth. "Then why are you bothering me, Denver?"

"I told you, I need a favor."

"What kind of favor?"

"The kind I don't want to share until you agree."

He puffed out a cloud of smoke. "I don't have time to get tied up in circular bullshit."

I pointed a finger at his holographic chest. "You owe me."

"Owe you for what?"

"The last case I took for you."

"The way I remember it, I paid you in full."

"Yeah, but I left my hazard pay off the bill, didn't I?"

"Hazard pay? What the hell? Somebody was killing my botsies, and I hired you to fix the problem. I paid—"

Nigel interrupted, "That was you?"

"It was her," said Jard.

"That was a scary time for all of us botsies," said Nigel. "Thank you, Denver."

I looked at Jard's holographic face and gestured in Nigel's direction as if to say *see*?

"You stay out of this, Nigel," said the pimp. "What I was starting to say, Denver, was you did a fine job, and I paid you every credit you asked for."

"You didn't give me any hazard pay."

"What hazard?"

"Dammit, Jard, you know I just about got dismembered by Rafe Ranchard."

"Is that what this is about? Is Rafe caught up in whatever trouble you're in?"

"Gods, I hope not. I've got enough trouble as it is. I only bring up Rafe to say that I risked my ass for you and your botsies. I think that earns me a favor."

Jard sucked on the cig-stick and sent a cloud out his nose. "Fine. What do you need?"

"You agree to help?"

"Yeah, I agree already. Now give me the details."

"I need you to get me into the shuttleport."

"The shuttleport? I don't know any pilots."

"I didn't say I needed a pilot. I have a friend inside who can help me. I just need to get past security."

"Then call your friend."

"I can't."

"Why not?"

"It's complicated."

"It's *always* complicated with you, Denver. What the hell makes you think I have any sway with shuttleport security?"

I put my hands on my hips and blew out a sigh. Jard and I both knew his business was ninety-nine percent sex trade, but a guy like Jard wasn't one to turn down requests for other services, and sneaking people in and out of the shuttleport was one of them.

"Can you get me in or not?"

I followed Nigel into an apartment complex. We ducked under clotheslines and entered a courtyard surrounded by dozens of small homes carved into rock. The smell of grilling meat added a pleasant aroma to the air that otherwise reeked of sulfur. Up a set of worn, rocky steps, we entered a small shop. No bigger than a bathroom, the shelves were stocked with dusty bottles and cellophane-wrapped snacks. The woman sitting on a stool greeted me with a quick lift of her eyebrows but nothing more.

Nigel handed her some credits and she poked at

her comm display. About thirty seconds later, a child appeared, perhaps five years old at most, her hair braided into tight cornrows.

Nigel rested a hand on the girl's shoulder. "This is Nina. All the shuttleport entrances are well guarded, so the coyotes dig their own tunnels, scores of them. When the authorities find one and dynamite it closed, the smugglers just dig another. The tunnels network in all directions, but Nina knows her way around; she'll get you in."

The girl reached for my hand and gripped two of my fingers. "Come," she said.

I wanted to tell her no. An adult should be taking me. Children didn't belong in the smuggling business, or any other business, especially one that was illegal and dangerous. But I was too desperate to argue. Let the quibbles over ethics fall to somebody else.

Mars was hard living, and a family like this was just filling a need. Who could blame them when there was so much money to be made off people who thought they could find a better life on one of the moons or in the belts? Earth was out of the question. That hellhole was dying and dying fast.

The girl gave my hand another tug. I looked at Nigel one last time, and he said, "I hope you find whoever you're looking for."

I did too. Navya and I hadn't parted on good terms

the last time we saw each other, but I didn't have any other options. She was the only pilot I knew.

"Safe travels, love," Nigel said.

I nodded my understanding to the botsie and let the girl lead me away into her home. We passed through a cramped kitchen, and then through a small living space populated by some old furniture. An elderly woman with wispy gray hair sat in a threadbare armchair. My eyes seized on the stone hanging from a chain around her neck, and my heart jumped into a higher gear.

<You see that stone, Smith?>

<Yes.>

<What color is it?>

<Color profile indicates aquamarine, Denver. Be on alert.>

An aquamarine gemstone was a common accessory of the Church of Mars, and if I'd been labeled an infidel, she might be calling the White Crusaders right now. The old woman stared at me the whole time, her face giving nothing away.

I exited the room. Nina brought me to a narrow staircase. "This way," she said before she raced to the top. I glanced over my shoulder before starting up after her. I took the steps slow so I could listen for any activity that might be happening behind me, but all I heard was the crinkle of plastic as Smith swung inside his bag.

At the top of the staircase was a long hallway. Nina was already ahead of me, so I picked up my pace. We entered a maintenance room of some sort. Tools hung on the walls and rusty appliances sat piled in the corner. I took another peek over my shoulder, but didn't see anybody following. Nina pointed at a short bookcase jammed with cans of paint.

"Push it," she said.

I moved to one end of the shelf and dropped a shoulder low. Pushing with my legs, the shelf began to slide. After two steps, a hole in the wall appeared. Nina crawled through even before the hole was fully exposed. I had to lay on my stomach and worm my way into the opening.

The tunnel was just tall enough to stand upright. Nina navigated the twists and turns with a lightbeam, and the deeper I went into the darkness, the more my paranoia started to fade. If that old woman had indeed called the White Crusade, they'd have a hell of a time trying to find me in this maze.

Nina led me from tunnel to tunnel, down service ladders, and at one point I had to hand-over-hand my way up a hanging rope with Nina riding piggyback. Finally, she led me to a wall of stone with a hole sitting at floor level. Very faint light beamed through to create a spot of warmth on the floor.

"The shuttleport?" I asked.

She nodded. "It's through there." Then she turned around and skipped away, her lightbeam bouncing wildly about until she disappeared around a corner. Again, I lay down, and passed Smith forward before wriggling my way into the hole. After moving under several inches of rock, I found myself crawling beneath a set of thick pipes. Pushing a few more inches, I entered a tight storeroom. Canned protein paste was stacked on shelves along with jarred vegetables and spices. A kitchen. Must've been one of the restaurants that served the port.

Nice work, Nina. This was the perfect place, considering the clothes I was wearing. I'd exit the restaurant looking like just another fry cook coming off her shift. From there, it shouldn't take me long to find Navya. I pulled myself off the floor and cracked the storeroom door. Not seeing anybody, I stepped into the kitchen, surprised to find it empty. My heart instantly kicked up a notch; a restaurant should be in the full swing of dinner service right now.

I walked to the far end of the kitchen, rounded a bend, and stopped at a door propped wide. Taking a tentative look through, my heart jumped into redline territory. The room was a vast sprawl of columns and arches and candlelit shrines. The lighting, I knew, was a dim, peaceful aquamarine.

<Uh-oh,> said the voice in my mind. <Looks like Nina led you into a trap.>

My eyes were already searching for the fastest way out of this church, but before I could locate the nearest exit, I heard footsteps and instinctively moved myself deeper into the doorway's shadow. Three monks appeared. And then a fourth. As if their minds were linked as one, they all picked up their pace, their sandals snapping loudly against the smooth stone floor.

I spun and darted back into the kitchen. If I could make it to the tunnels, I'd have a good chance of losing them in the dark labyrinth. I entered the kitchen at top speed and aimed for the storeroom, but the door was guarded by two more monks with weapons pointed at me.

Shit!

<Take cover, Denver!> Smith screamed into my brain.

I put on the brakes and skidded to the floor behind an oven. Disruptor fire tore into the wall behind me. I reached into the take-out bag, grasped Smith's handle and tossed the bag aside. The monks fired again. I pointed Smith over the top of the oven in the direction of the oncoming fire.

<If you see one, take 'em out,> I said.

I felt a tingle in the back of my mind as if Smith silently nodded his understanding.

He tracked the closest target and unleashed a pulse of energy. The monk's skull exploded, the blast vaporizing everything above his jaw.

<Got him!> Smith said.

Another round of fire came at us. Heat from one of the blasts singed my exposed hand, and I nearly dropped my pistol.

"Son of a bitch!" I said and pulled Smith back behind the oven with me.

<More closing in, Denver. This isn't looking good…>

Smith's eyepiece gave him a 360-degree view that allowed him to map most of the area, even behind cover. Another round of shots punched holes into our position. Steel shelving sparked and gnarled and tipped forward. I scrambled as it dumped stacks of pots and pans to the floor with a deafening racket.

<Find us a way out!>

<Working on it. Hang tight and keep your head low.>

<Thanks for the advice.>

I crawled under a table and found cover behind a freezer chest. Pressing my back against the steel, I listened for approaching enemies. The room was quiet now. The monks had probably taken cover themselves and were busy formulating a plan of attack.

<You aren't going to like this, Denver.>

<What? Spit it out!>

<None of my simulations give us a way out. There are six of them against one of you. I recommend surrender.>

Another three blasts pounded the wall behind me.

<Hell no.>

<I knew you'd say that. Are you sure I can't convince you?>

<Smith!>

<Alright then, get ready.>

A cold sting pinched my right palm as Smith injected me with stims.

The drug took hold, and I instantly felt my heart and lungs jam into overdrive. My vision blurred for a moment and then began to sharpen. Every item in my view came into exquisite focus.

The pistol in my hand began to transform. The barrel slid forward and tipped down to form a second handhold. The hammer popped back and a power pack unfolded with a click and a hum. From the power pack, a new barrel telescoped forward and snapped into place.

Smith counted six monks total, but a pulse cannon went a long way toward evening the odds. I took a quick glance and saw a bald head peeking past the stove. I fired. A pulse rippled outward, expanding in diameter as it did. Plates and silverware jumped off a table, and then the table itself leapt up and blew apart. I crawled to the far end of the freezer chest. The storeroom was just a few feet away, but there was nothing but open space between here and there. I looked back to see if anybody was closing from behind. I didn't see anyone, but I sent a pulse in that general direction anyway. Shrapnel from kitchen equipment embedded itself in the stone walls.

I nudged an eye past the edge of the freezer chest again. The walk-in refrigerator door was open and I could see two pairs of feet huddled behind it. A blast at them could buy me the time I needed to run for the storeroom, but the sound of sandals scuffing across metal gave me pause. At least one of the monks had climbed up on top of one of the ovens, which meant he or she had a clear line of sight to the storeroom door.

Disruptor fire pounded the lights over my head and I closed my eyes against the rain of glass and sparks tumbling down. The freezer took a shot, and I felt it buck against my back. I peeked at the storeroom again, knowing it was too late. All six monks had settled into position and had me pinned in a vicious crossfire. If I ran, I'd be blown apart. Staying where I was, it was only a matter of time before the freezer chest crumbled to leave me exposed.

I was screwed.

CHAPTER ELEVEN

ONE OF THE FREEZER CHEST'S HINGES TORE FREE, bolts shooting off like bullets. The lid sat cockeyed as disruptor fire continued to blast away. I reached my arms tall as I could over the freezer to take a couple pot shots, but the pulses didn't stop the incessant barrage on my position.

<Any ideas, Smith?>

<No, Denver. I'm sorry. But choose your next shots carefully, my battery is getting low.>

<Turn your transmitter on. Broadcast everything we have to as many people as possible. If we can't rescue Ojiisan, maybe somebody else will.>

The words tasted bitter even as I spoke them in my mind. Ojiisan had sent me a message. A cry for help. And I'd failed him.

Smoke stung my eyes, and I looked to the storeroom door one more time in hopes there might be enough of it to cover my sprint. But no, the haze was, at best, thick enough to shroud a ghost. All five and a half feet of me? Not a chance.

Then a figure appeared in the storeroom, and I had to blink to make sure I wasn't imagining it. He stood in the doorway, rubbing his chin as he surveyed the situation. Disruptor fire continued to pummel the freezer chest. The monks were so focused on me, they hadn't noticed him.

<Belay that order, Smith.>

<Transmission on hold.>

I stayed low and gathered my feet under me. My eyes stayed riveted as I prepared for the shortest, fastest sprint of my life. The figure moved deeper into the storeroom and came back to the doorway with a can of protein paste. He winked at me before lifting the can high and throwing it as hard as he could. I sped in his direction. From the corner of my eye, I saw a monk fall from his perch, a spray of blood erupting from his scalp.

The disruptor fire stopped as the monks tried to figure out what had just happened. Smith drained his power to zero sending out a few more havoc-creating pulses. The figure moved aside to let me through. Throwing Smith ahead of me, I dove for the hole in the wall. I hit the ground hard and my breath was pushed from my lungs in a whoosh. I started to wriggle forward, but with the wind knocked out of me, I wasn't making much distance. Then I felt a hand grab my belt and, with a toss, I tumbled into the tunnel.

I was still trying to fill my lungs when the figure came through, followed by a spray of splinters from the exploding storeroom door.

Grabbing me again by the belt, he hefted me like a suitcase and ran into the dark.

"Nice to see you again, love," he said.

CHAPTER TWELVE

THE LIGHTBEAM BOBBED LEFT AND RIGHT AS Nigel and I marched farther and farther away from the church. My head pounded as the stims wore off.

"I followed you," he said.

"So I figured. Thank you."

"Thank Jard. He asked me to keep an eye on you."

"I will," I said with genuine gratitude. Owing my life to a pimp and scoundrel like Jard was a tough pill to swallow, but at the moment I didn't care. If he were here, I'd give the bastard a kiss.

But it really was Nigel who deserved the gratitude. His jacket was peppered with holes from blasts he'd taken in our escape. If it weren't for him, those holes would be in my head.

Nigel aimed his lightbeam at a ladder. "This way."

"Are you sure?"

"No, but I think the shuttleport has to be up, don't you? It's built on a plateau."

"It's not a very tall plateau."

"True, but I still think it's up."

I shrugged and handed Smith to Nigel before starting up the rungs. Making it to the top, I reached down through the hole so Nigel could toss the gun up to me. Smith was still in a very inconvenient cannon mode. He wouldn't be able to transform back to an easy-to-carry pistol until he got a recharge.

"So why do you want to leave Mars?" asked Nigel.

"Who said I want to leave?"

"Why else are you trying to smuggle yourself into the shuttleport?"

"I need to find my grandfather."

"You need a shuttle for that?"

"I do."

Ahead, I could see white light beaming down through the ceiling. We moved toward the brightness and stopped directly underneath. Overhead was a metal floor grate like the kind used in ventilation systems. Only we weren't inside a ventilation system. "Must be a dummy," I said.

"Bloody clever."

I reached high and laced my fingers through the grating. Pulling myself upward, I pressed an eye against the metal. The room above was so large I couldn't see any walls. The ceiling was a towering crisscross of metal struts. "That's a massive space," I said. "It has to be the shuttleport."

The telltale screech of engines firing up confirmed it. I let go and dropped back to the floor. The engines got louder, and I plugged my ears against the deafening wail. Vibrations reverbed through my chest as a shadow replaced the light. Nigel and I watched a shuttle roll by, flashing lights pulsing from the metal plating. A thick black tire wheeled in and out of view, and then a series of numbers written in phosphorescent paint.

The vibrations in my skull felt like they were going to blow my head apart as the aft engine pounded us with a furnace blast of white hot energy. I felt it ripple down my body, lighting every nerve with an unpleasant itch. Finally, the ship was past, and I pulled my hands from over my ears.

"Dammit. We need to find another way in," I said.

"Can't you call the shuttle pilot? They can park overhead and you can go right up and in through the emergency hatch. Nobody would see a thing."

"I don't have a shuttle booked. And I can't get on the comm system or they'll trace my location."

"No shuttle? What were you going to do when you got inside? You're not a hijacker, are you?"

"No, not yet."

"Very well," he said. "Let's find another way."

We sat in a bar located in the shuttleport perimeter that was closed off to anyone without proper clearance.

Nigel found the tunnel that got us inside. He'd tossed the tie and jacket and had his entire torso exposed. His physique was impressive. In almost every way, he looked human. But it wouldn't be enough. He'd have to find a better disguise soon if we hoped to avoid looking suspicious to shuttleport security.

"So how long are we going to sit here?" he asked.

I tapped my hip, where Smith—back in pistol mode—was tucked into my belt and hidden under my shirt. "Until he gets a full charge. Or until Navya walks by. Whichever comes first."

"How do you know she'll walk by?"

I took a sip of my drink and kept my eyes aimed at the street outside. "I don't. But this is the closest bar to the exit. She must take the tram home from work. That means that after her shift, she should walk right by this place."

"But what if she's out on a trip? If she runs the cargo route to the orbital platform like you say, then she could be out for a day or more at a time."

"You could be right. I'm just hoping to catch a break."

"We're the only ones here. The waitress keeps giving us the eye. They want to close up for the night."

"She just doesn't like the way you're dressed."

"That too. So how much longer?"

<Smith?>

<Sixty-seven percent. The wireless charging is slow here. I estimate thirty-three minutes to full charge.>

"Another half hour," I said to Nigel.

"But the waitress, she—"

"Thirty more minutes," I said, enunciating each word.

"But if—"

"You know, I've had a hell of a day. If you don't like my decisions, then you should go."

"I'm just trying to help. Jard told me to keep an eye on you."

"If you want to help, then sit there and be quiet." I turned my gaze back on the window that faced the street. Hardly anybody was out anymore. The hour was very late.

Nigel stayed silent, his lips pinched, his foot tapping at the floor.

<You should apologize,> said Smith.

<What for?>

<You hurt his feelings.>

<He's a botsie. He doesn't have feelings.>

<You know that's not true, Denver. Jard's bots are very advanced. You saw some amazing things when you worked that case for him.>

He was right about that. I saw things I didn't think were possible. A botsie and a human who appeared to truly love each other. Botsies who were willing to sacrifice for one another. A botsie who had become disturbed in an all too human way.

<Tell him you're sorry,> said Smith. <Without him you wouldn't have found the shuttleport or the tunnel that got us inside.>

Nigel's head was tipped forward, blank eyes aimed at the floor. Without him, I'd be dead.

"Nigel, I'm sorry." I stood and dropped some credits on the table. He looked at me, his eyes unreadable. I put a hand on his shoulder and offered a soft squeeze. "You're right. We should go."

He nodded and stood. "We can spend the night in the tunnels and try to find her again in the morning."

Exiting the bar, we walked a short distance to a sparsely populated corridor, and I saw a woman a few doors down holding a sign. Thinking she must be Church of Mars, I was about to suggest we take a different route to avoid her, but then I read the sign. *ALIENS WALK AMONG US.* Just a regular crazy instead of a religious crazy.

"Security's tight here. I'm surprised they let these whackos inside," I said.

"Maybe she came in the same way we did," Nigel said.

We passed her and a few closed-for-the-night storefronts before entering the showers. The shuttleport had three different public showers with corresponding locker rooms for pilots and maintenance workers. This one just happened to have a hidden entry behind the water heaters, which was how we got in.

Passing co-ed lockers and hampers full of musty-smelling wet towels, Nigel spotted an open closet with various gear hanging inside. He nabbed a shirt and a pilot's jacket and put them on. We made our way down a long hallway when I spotted a woman in a black shirt and black pants drying her hair in front of a mirror. I stopped dead in my tracks. "Navya?"

Unable to hear me, I had to tap on her shoulder. She found my reflection in the mirror and turned off the dryer. "Yes?"

"It's me. Denver."

"Oh." Navya gazed over her shoulder at me, an annoyed look on her face. "What happened to your hair?" Then she eyed my grease-stained clothes. "You finally got yourself a real job, I see. About time."

"I need your help," I said.

She flicked the dryer on and turned back to the mirror.

Nigel leaned my way. "I thought you said she was a friend."

"She was. She is. She's just mad at me."

"For what?"

I tapped her shoulder again. Again the dryer turned off. "Listen, Navya, I need a shuttle."

"So go buy a ticket."

"I need a shuttle to take me south. Far south."

"Like I said, buy a damn ticket."

"This has to be on the down low. There are people after me. I can't have my name on any of the logs."

Navya set the dryer down and leaned against the counter. "Why should I care? And who is this guy?"

"This is Nigel," I said. He tipped his head in

greeting. "I need your help, Navya. I can pay whatever rate you charge."

"The hell you can." She crossed her arms. "You can't afford me or my rig."

I took a deep breath. "That may be true, but I'll pay you back. I wouldn't come to you like this if I had another choice."

Navya laughed at that. "You had no choice? Where have I heard that before?"

"What could I do, Navya? He was fixing pit fights."

She pointed a finger. "You didn't have to do what you did."

"Julio was scamming Joanna Petrovic herself. She would've found out eventually, and what would've happened to him then? What would've happened when the most ruthless kingpin on Mars found out your boyfriend was stealing tens of thousands of credits from under her nose?"

Navya shook her head. "You conned that fighter into not taking a dive like he was supposed to. Julio bet everything he had, and you completely zeroed him out."

I leaned forward and aimed a hard gaze at my former friend. "I saved his life is what I did. If I hadn't torpedoed his little scam, his head would be impaled on one of her bedposts, and I mean that literally.

"Besides," I said in a softer tone, "he was cheating on you, and let's not forget that's why you asked me to follow him in the first place."

"That's not the point," she said, her finger pointing at me again. "You didn't talk to me. You didn't tell me shit. You just did what you wanted. Ever since we were teenagers, that's what you've always done."

I looked at Nigel, who was nodding his head. "Yes," he said, "she can be very single-minded."

I threw up my hands. "Really, Nigel? You know me so well after half a day?"

"Just an observation, love."

Smith's voice sounded in my head. <Now that he mentions it...>

<You shut the hell up.>

I turned back to Navya. Her arms were crossed tight, her shoulders hiked in frustration. She stared at me, her eyes edged by angled eyebrows.

"I'm sorry," I told her. "I should've talked to you first."

Her face didn't budge from its stern pose, and I knew if I was going to find Ojiisan, I had to face the truth. "I screwed up, Navya. I didn't realize I was going to hurt you." I touched a hand to my heart. "I should've talked to you first."

"Yes, you should've, dammit." She wiped her suddenly cloudy eyes. "You're such an asshole. You know that?"

"I know," I said as I stepped forward and wrapped my arms around her shoulders. I leaned my forehead against hers. "I know."

Her shoulders softened under my grasp, and I felt

her arms uncross and reach around me to complete the embrace.

"I'm sorry," I said.

"You better be." Gently, she pushed me back. "Now what the hell trouble are you in? What are you doing here?"

"I need you to take me to Ojiisan."

CHAPTER THIRTEEN

I SAT NEXT TO NAVYA, NIGEL STANDING BEHIND me, his hands on the back of my seat. Days had passed, a full seventy-two hours of unbearably tense boredom. Nigel and I spent the entire time hiding in Navya's shuttle, me surviving on emergency rations and whatever leftovers Navya was nice enough to bring aboard while Nigel juiced himself up every so often by sitting under the recharging station.

We'd been stowaways for two runs up to the orbital platform, where huge interplanetary cargo-liners docked to exchange goods and credits. We'd been biding our time until today, the first day Navya's shuttle service was free of any bookings.

Navya drove the shuttle to the launch pad and slowly lifted us from the ground. A hundred meters ahead, I watched gears crank and pistons stretch. Slowly, eight gigantic triangular doors, like slices of a massive steel pie, started to part and lever inward. Another ship pulled alongside us as the huge doors worked themselves fully open, exposing a half dozen shuttles floating inside. The ships eased from the airlock and edged downward to pass directly below our position.

Clearance granted, Navya pushed us forward. We inched through the doors and into the airlock, a giant cavern lit by broad batteries of white lights. Traffic control personnel sat behind a row of windows speaking into microphones. Behind them was a wall lit with stats and maps and animations. I adjusted my sungoggles and stayed low in my seat to keep from calling attention to myself.

Navya moved us close to the exit, and we waited for two other ships to come inside and hover in loose formation. The doors we'd come through closed with a clang that shook my seat. Warning lights began to flash, and ceiling vents slowly opened. The shuttle shook as air gusted from the airlock out into Mars' burgeoning atmosphere. Puffs of sand blew in through the vents to drift and sparkle in the bright lights. The ceiling's steel doors began to iris, and a whoosh of sand pelted our windshield. The shuttle rose, and once outside visibility dropped to complete zero inside spiraling maelstroms of sand.

Navya kept her eyes on her display, on the dots that represented the other two ships lifting into the sky. When one of the dots started to blink, she moved the yoke to create more space. The dot stopped blinking again as the sandstorms thinned to the point that I could see five, maybe ten meters ahead, and then then we were out of it. The sky stretched to impossible distances, where stars were trapped like diamond dust on black velvet.

<Enhance me?>

<Yes,> said Smith. <It's too beautiful to be limited to black and white.>

My view went dark for a few seconds as he colorized the imagery he received through my eyes. Beaming it back to me, the entire scene blossomed in my mind. Colors soaked into view and I sucked in a breath at the beauty before me. The sandstorms below boiled and whirled, spinning off stunning eddies of rust and cinnamon that dissipated as quickly as they were spawned.

The two second delay between moving my eyes and seeing the colorized version made me sick on most occasions, but it was perfect for a time like this, a time when I was staring in one direction into the distance, a time when I didn't want to miss the subtle variations between brushstrokes of paprika and cayenne.

We banked and Navya set us on a heading that was very close to due south. Smith reverted my vision back to monochrome to avoid the side effects I was prone to once we started moving. I reached a hand to Navya's shoulder. "Thank you."

She nodded. "I know how much he meant to you."

I'd expected plenty of argument. How do you know he's not dead? After all these years you really think you know where he is? How can you be so sure? But she hadn't asked any of those questions. Once I'd apologized, she took the rest of it in stride. "Of course, I'll help," was what she said.

I should've apologized straight away. I shouldn't have let it fester for six months. But I did. Why being right was so damned important to me, I didn't know.

Navya stayed focused on the screen until the other bright dots faded from view, and we were alone. "Nine hours and eleven minutes."

Nine hours until I'd find my grandfather and bring him home.

"So, Nigel," said Navya. "Any ideas what to do with all that time?"

"What did you have in mind, love?"

"There's a fold-down passenger bed in the cargo hold."

"Now that sounds bloody fascinating. Can you show me?"

Navya stood up and gave me a broad grin, her cheeks already flushing. "You can let me know if anything starts buzzing, can't you, Denver?"

I nodded.

Navya stepped to the ladder and practically hopped onto the rungs. I watched her descend, and Nigel follow her down, offering me a wink before he disappeared below decks.

Nine hours.

CHAPTER FOURTEEN

THE HOURS TICKED BY SO SLOW THEY SEEMED TO stretch into days. Not since my sunrise ceremony had I experienced time crawling at such a glacial pace.

The journey ahead of us was nearly as vast as the landscape. I jumped out of monochrome to help pass the time. Despite the aid of Smith's colorization, the scenery had long since become monotonous. Other than catching a nice glimpse of the immense Olympus Mons in the distance, the view was nothing but reds. Even the occasional break in the storms offered little more than a different texture painted with the same color palette.

I checked the clock. Still an hour to go. Navya was back at the helm. After three trips to the cargo hold—three!—she'd settled into her pilot's seat for the rest of the trip. We stilted attempts at catching up on the months we'd not been speaking to each other until she decided to ride in silence. To her credit, she hadn't shown any signs of being offended. She knew how dire my situation was.

She knew I'd taken a chance that Ojiisan was still alive, and as sure as I was that I could feel his presence deep in my heart, it was still a chance.

And even if I did find him, what would I do then? Where would I take him? I couldn't take him home, where Hennessey would be waiting to assassinate us both. What if Ojiisan wasn't well? What if he needed a doctor?

The questions gnawed ruthlessly at my mind. At my sanity. And at my resolve.

Still, the countdown timer continued to descend. When it ticked under a half hour, we finally passed beyond the sandstorms to see the rocky surface unimpeded. Other than the occasional dust devil, the scenery was impossibly still. Motion sickness started to set in, so I told Smith to turn off the colorization and Mars bleached before my eyes, reds and oranges becoming slate and gunmetal.

Trimming the altitude, we skimmed over hills and valleys, craters and crevices, the surface of Mars a coarse mix of sand and rubble. The timer ticked under ten minutes, and I shook off the slightest sense of dizziness and stood for a better view as we descended into a shallow canyon. Walls of rock crowded all sides as Navya guided us through, the ship tilting slightly along with the gentle turns.

Nigel appeared next to me, his arm reaching over my shoulder and pulling me close. "I hope he's here," he said.

I leaned into the hug. "Thanks."

The canyon spilled into a vast plane, its surface rippled by dunes that resembled an ocean of waves. I gripped the co-pilot's chair as I searched for structures or tents or anything that could support life, my grandfather's life.

"There," I said, my finger pointing at a black dot in the distance.

"I see it," said Navya. At the same moment, a blip appeared on her nav display. "It's a ship."

A ship? Could he have crash landed out here? Could the life support system of a disabled ship keep him alive this long?

Gradually the dot grew into a spot, and the spot into a set of blocky lines. The ship was small, less than half the size of Navya's cargo shuttle. Big enough to support a small scouting party, but that was about it.

"Recognize it?" I asked.

Navya shook her head. "It's old. Looks like one of the exploration ships they used after colonizing."

My heart swelled with hope. I'm here Ojiisan. I've found you.

"There's a bunker," said Nigel. Straining my eyes, I could barely make out a dark shape, hard edges standing out against a backdrop of the dunes' smooth curves.

Navya tapped on her display screen. "Um, this can't be right."

"What?" I asked, feeling a nervous pull in my gut.

"The ship; its engines are live."

I struggled to interpret what she'd said. If he was marooned, the ship's engines should be dead.

"Not just live," said Navya. "Sensors show it's powering for takeoff."

"Can you call them?"

Navya punched some controls and spoke into the command console. "Attention unidentified vessel, this is Firestar on the guard channel, do you copy? Repeat, this is Firestar on guard, do you copy? Over."

Static came back through the radio and Navya tried again.

"Looks like they're ignoring us," she said.

"Dammit!" I shouted. "We have to hurry. Can you block their takeoff?"

"I can try, but—"

"Do it! Get us over there! Don't let them leave."

Our shuttle surged, and I held tight onto the seatback to keep from falling. Nigel took a step back to regain his balance.

Navya grabbed her seatbelt and snapped it into place. "Belt up! When I get overtop, I'll reverse the engines as hard as I can. So hold onto something."

I dropped into the seat next to her and slapped my belt into place. Behind me, Nigel belted into a fold-down seat.

"People on the surface," said Navya. "Three of them heading for the ship."

I saw them. They crested a dune about halfway

between the bunker and the ship. Two of them wore dark colored enviro-suits, their helmet lights shining bright. The third's suit was a lighter color and the helmet had a narrow face-shield in the style of the original colonizers. Ojiisan!

Navya hit the fore thrusters and the ship slammed into a wall of deceleration. My seat belt clawed into my chest and gut, and I instinctively reached a bracing hand for the dashboard. Stressed, the shuttle rattled as we closed on the other ship, its hull disappearing under ours.

Navya cut altitude until we heard the wrenching clunk of the two hulls making contact. She worked the controls, her eyes glued to the gauges. "I'll do my best to keep most of the weight off them so I don't collapse their landing struts. They're going to be *pissed*, but they're not going anywhere. You better be right about all of this, Denver."

The three figures outside were moving fast now, descending the dune with long loping strides. I pressed my palm against the windshield and whispered, "Ojiisan, it's me."

The radio squawked into life. "Get the hell off us!"

The voice, I knew it. I knew *him*. "Who are you?" asked Navya. "What are you doing down there?"

"None of your damn business."

I struggled to put a name to the voice. Hennessey was the obvious choice, but the voice on the radio lacked

Hennessey's measured deliberation. This voice was angry. Feral.

No way. "Rafe Ranchard, is that you?" I pounded the windshield with a fist as the three figures reached the bottom of the dune and my grandfather disappeared from view to board the ship below.

Navya was speaking into the radio, but I cut her off.

"Let him go, Rafe. Let him go now or we'll turn off our boosters and squash you into the dirt. Then nobody's leaving."

"The quarry is coming on board now. Get off us, or I'll kill him."

Navya lifted questioning eyebrows, but I stopped her with a sharp wave of my hand. I needed to think.

Rafe Ranchard. The man was capital-P psychotic. Hennessey's former right-hand man.

Rafe had once been Hennessey's star preacher, a fundamentalist fanatic with the talent to swell the ranks. He originally made his name attacking the evils of the botsie trade, but pretty soon, he had a hard-on for sins of all kinds. He was so successful he even started his very own sect inside the Church of Mars. Until I came along and his position was revoked.

And now, of all places, he was here. And he had my grandfather.

"You know who this is, Rafe?" I asked.

"He's inside, and I've got a chisel up to his throat, Denver. Let us go or I'll kill him."

"No," I said, my voice surprisingly calm. "Put his helmet back on and send him outside. When I see he's safe, we'll let you go, and *I'll* be the one to pick him up."

He brushed off my demands with a laugh. "Nothing would give me more pleasure than to run this chisel through his windpipe. You know the only reason I haven't already done it is because I can't see your face. Turn on the holo and let me get a good look at you."

"Listen to me, Rafe, I don't know why you're running Hennessey's errands, but you're not leaving with my grandfather."

"Hennessey? I don't do his dirty work anymore. He excommunicated me, remember?"

I did. Call Hennessey a louse and a backstabber, but he knew a threat to his own power when he saw one, and some accounting irregularities were all it took to get Rafe a one-way ticket to excommunication.

His voice slithered through the speakers. "And don't you dare forget how you helped him do it, Denver. You're the one who said I was embezzling."

"That was what the financials showed, Rafe."

"I know damn well what they showed. I know better than anybody. You should've dug deeper. You should've seen the records were doctored. You're a damned investigator, right? Hennessey brought you and your famous name in to validate his bullshit, and you just rubber stamped it all with barely a glance. You didn't give two shits if it ruined a righteous man's career as long as you got paid, right?"

"All I did was follow the evidence. Like I told you the last time we met, where it led is your problem, not mine."

"The last time we met, yes. It really should've been the *last time*."

No doubt about that. I almost died that day in the mine. Three of his henchmen weren't so lucky. "Listen, Rafe, what's in the past is in the past. What matters right now is my grandfather. Let me talk to him."

"You want to talk to him? Give me a second."

Surprised to have won the concession, I waited nervously to hear if the impossible was actually true, that his death was a cruel fiction, and his imprisonment in that bunker outside was crueler still.

"Here," said Rafe, "say hello to your granddaughter."

I leaned forward, my shoulders so tense they ached. "Ojiisan?"

"Hello," said a voice heavy with the gravel of age. Twenty years might've passed, but I instantly knew it was the same voice that read to me when I was a child. The same voice that woke me up when it was time for school. It was *him*.

My eyes misted over. "It's me, Ojiisan. It's Denver. I've come a long way to find you. I know you're scared, but I'm here to bring you home."

When he spoke, his tone sounded tentative. Confused. "Who did you say you were?"

My heart dropped in my chest, and the first tear broke free and ran down my cheek. "It's me, Ojiisan. Your granddaughter. It's Denver."

"Granddaughter? I'm sorry, but I don't know who you are..."

Rafe's laughter came through the speaker loud and long. The harsh sound ricocheted off the cockpit to crash against the walls of my skull. "You know, Denver," he said, "I never thought I'd say this, but right now, I'm glad you slipped away from me last time. I wouldn't miss this for the world."

I opened my mouth, but I had no words.

"He doesn't remember anything," said Rafe. "My people talked to him for an hour in that bunker of his, and he doesn't even know his own name."

I sank deep into my seat. My mouth was still open and I practically had to use my fist to shove it closed.

"You're awfully quiet, Denver. You didn't lose your memory too, now did you?"

"Why are you here, asshole? What do you want with him?"

"It's not me who wants him. It's Hennessey. He's the one who stashed him away down here. And now that I've got him, you can bet your ass Hennessey will be playing by my rules."

"Why would Hennessey do that? Why exile him?"

"How would I know? You're the investigator. All I

know is Hennessey kept this little secret for twenty years, and I bet he wants to keep it a little longer."

"How did you find him?"

"What you really want to know is how did I find him *first*? Maybe I should be the one with the detective business."

"How? Tell me!"

"The church, Denver. When I was the finance officer, there wasn't an expense I didn't see, and every six months the Peerless Leader himself personally approved a supply run to this area of the planet. I never knew why, but when messages started popping up from your long-lost grandfather, I took a guess that maybe, just maybe, the great Tatsuo Moon would be here, and I was right."

"Let me have him, Rafe."

"Keep dreaming, Denver. When I bring this prize back home, Hennessey will have no choice but to reinstate me. That, or his little secret will go public. That man is slick as shit in the rain, but he'll have a hell of a time trying to explain this one away."

"You hate Hennessey. Why the hell do you want back into the church?"

"Don't you see? The old man is going to need a successor, and when I take back my rightful place as his number two, I'll be first in line to become Peerless Leader when he dies. And mark my words, when I get my chance to stand by his side, that unfortunate day might come a lot sooner than you think. So how about you move aside and let me be on my way?"

"Not a chance."

"I'll kill him, Denver. I doubt Hennessey will care if his head is attached or not when I hand it over."

"You turn him over to me or we'll crush that ship of yours."

"And kill your precious Ojiisan in the process? I don't think so."

"We're not moving."

"You can't stay there forever."

"We'll wait you out if we have to. Our holds are a lot bigger than yours and ours are full of food and water."

Navya nodded her approval of the lie.

He was quiet for a bit. Long enough that I thought he might actually be considering letting Ojiisan go.

The alarms were loud and sudden, and I jumped from my seat enough to feel the bite of my belt. Air gusted from the cockpit. The floor had a hole in it, and so did the ceiling, both the size of a fist. I stared at one of the holes wondering what could possibly punch through two decks of steel. Masks dropped from the ceiling, and Navya slipped hers on. I fumbled with the straps of my own mask for a moment before Nigel grabbed hold and took care of it for me.

I took a deep breath as Rafe's voice bellowed with the accusatory power of a preacher in hellfire sermon. "Flee or suffer the wrath! Purge the sins lest they devour you!"

Our ship rocked again and another pair of holes appeared. What the hell?

Navya slapped the controls, and we were in motion. The grind of metal on metal was barely audible over the whine of fans trying but failing to keep the cabin pressurized. She swung the nose around fast to bring Rafe's ship back into view. It was already lifting off, two suited figures hanging on to the ladder.

Navya pointed the nose downward, preparing to land. I grabbed her wrist and shook my head, my voice sounding strange in the thin air. "We have to go after them!"

She shook her head. "We'll never make it." She dropped the landing struts and put us on the ground.

I watched Rafe's ship shrink to a dot and then a speck and then disappear. I slammed my fists into the armrests. "Dammit!"

I dropped my face into my hands and noticed a tripod on the ground. Mounted atop was something akin to a harpoon. Smith spoke into my mind. <It's a depth charger. That thing can drive a hole twenty meters into solid rock. Throw some high-powered explosives in the hole, and they can blast apart the most stubborn stones.>

<Thanks for the lesson.> I should've seen it coming. In his second career, Rafe had become a miner. He probably lifted that ship from Blevin's Mine, which meant it was an explorer, likely loaded with mining gear. All that

talk was just intended to keep me occupied while his crew set up the depth charger in our shadow.

"How could I have been so stupid?" I said.

Nigel put a hand on my shoulder, "It's okay, love. None of us expected that."

"I should've known better."

I hung my head and started to shiver from the cold. Navya was already suiting up. I stayed where I was, my body going as numb as my mind. Nigel unbuckled my belt and pulled me upright. He grabbed an enviro-suit and held it for me to step into. I willed my legs to move, dropping one foot inside and then the other.

I nodded my thanks and waved Nigel away. I could do the rest. Ojiisan was alive, and if we were going to go get him, this ship needed to be patched and fast.

CHAPTER FIFTEEN

I LEFT NIGEL AND NAVYA IN THE ENGINE ROOM and went back outside. The patch job was done, but one of the overworked ventilation fans failed and required a new power supply. Re-pressurize in one hour, depart ten minutes later was the latest estimate, if everything went smoothly.

I climbed the dune my grandfather descended two hours ago, his footprints still clear in the sand. Reaching the top, I headed through a small field of solar panels to stand in front of the bunker. Steel walls rose three or four feet from the sand to form a box with a hatch on the ceiling. Using a crate as a step, I climbed to the top.

The hatch had been left open, and I descended the ladder. I needed to see the place my grandfather had been living for all these years. Passing through a very compact airlock, I continued to descend until my boots dropped to the floor.

The bunker was tiny. Like the cabin of an elevator.

The walls were rock and cold steel. Same for the floor. The bed was a shelf and a threadbare blanket. The toilet was a bucket.

Twenty years, Hennessey had put him here. Alone. Without even his memory to keep him company.

I'd make the bastard pay.

The trip home was tediously long. I sat in the co-pilot's chair, my foot tapping mercilessly at the floor. Every so often, Navya or Nigel would ask what my plan was when we arrived, and I always gave the same answer. *I don't know.*

Go to the media? Go to the ministry of police? Go to Doctor Werner?

Who were my allies? Who were enemies?

What I wanted to do was go to Rafe's mine, put a hole between his eyes, and rescue my grandfather, but I knew how incredibly vast that mine had grown after fifteen years in service. Ojiisan could be anywhere inside that warren of tunnels and shafts. Without an army, searching was impossible.

Smith was silent the entire way. More than once, I'd thought about checking in with him, but decided to leave him alone with his thoughts. Hearing the voice of my grandfather, the man whose memories he'd integrated, might've been a bigger shock to him than it was to me.

Finally, we approached Mars City. It was the dark of

night, and the storms were quiet for a change, yet the air was still thick with haze. Our lights pierced the gloom to illuminate hulking wrecks of gnarled steel. Some had tipped over and others still reached upward like trees of an ancient forest back on Earth. The builders.

Ahead, glowing domes showed faintly through the murk. Navya spoke on the radio, seeking clearance to enter the shuttleport. Her display screen was dark and quiet. No ships anywhere nearby.

The response came back from flight control, the voice cutting in and out, and then going completely silent. A light blinked into existence just ahead of us. "Who the hell is that?" asked Navya as she changed course to give it broad leeway.

My heart was already kicking into overdrive when another light lit on her screen, and another.

"They're lifting from the surface!" shouted Navya as she jerked us hard to the left. She tried the radio again. "They're jamming communications."

A spotlight shone straight through the windshield to blind us with bright white light. I shielded my eyes to look at Navya's display screen. We were surrounded.

CHAPTER SIXTEEN

GRAPPLERS, DOZENS OF THEM, PINGED AGAINST the hull. The ship lurched side to side as thick cables cranked taut. Navya tried to wrench us free, but I knew it was of no use. Whoever they were, they had us trapped.

"Bloody hell, you live a complicated life," Nigel said as he stared into the beam of the spotlight.

Shadows moved overhead. I looked up to see black figures coming down the grappling cables. Like spiders descending a silk, their approach was silent until their boots landed upon the windshield to smudge the glass with their treads.

Navya shut down all the thrusters, and I felt the ship sag into its web. A light flashed to show the airlock had been entered.

"We have visitors," said Navya. "Since when are you so popular?"

"Maybe they're here for me," said Nigel dryly. "My regulars must be missing me by now."

Taking Smith off my lap, I set him on the floor. I couldn't fight my way out of this one. I stood and faced the door, Navya and Nigel lining up to either side of me.

The door opened, and in stepped a trio of suited figures. The bright light from the spotlight outside glared off their faceshields. Their suits were solid black, no markings to give away who they were.

One of them gestured for us to raise our hands. A quick frisk and, after collecting Smith from the floor, he returned to his group.

One of the other two stepped forward and unbuckled the latches of his helmet. Twisting the helmet, he pulled it free from the neck ring and lifted it off his bald head.

The other monks removed their own helmets and helped the Peerless Leader with his gloves. "Wherever you stashed him," Hennessey said, "we'll find him. I have a dozen people searching every inch of this ship."

"So, it's true. You were behind it all," I said.

"Believe me, Denver, the situation is far more complicated than you could ever imagine."

"We don't have him."

Hennessey shook his head. "Come now, Denver, you expect me to believe you left him there?"

"Believe me now or believe me after you finish your search. It's up to you."

His brows cinched for a moment as it began to dawn on him that I might be telling the truth. "Where is he?"

I stared at the Peerless Leader as he waited for an

answer, his eyes calm and showing no sign of guilt or shame. Heat rose up from my chest into my neck and cheeks. "Why did you do it? Why did you tell everybody he died? Why did you lock him up and erase his memory?"

He crossed his arms. "You don't know him as well as you think you do, Denver. Can't say I blame you for that. You were just a little girl back then. I was there the day you were born, you know. I knew Tatsuo far longer than you did. He was so proud to be a grandfather. It wasn't a year later when he had to take you in. Do you even remember your parents?"

I shook my head.

"Tragic what happened to them, and I really mean that. Nobody deserves to die like that, to die at the hands of a feve-ravaged gunman. Can't you see what a scourge red fever is? Or does that immunity of yours blind you to more than colors?"

"This has nothing to do with the feve. This is about Ojiisan and what you did to him."

"It has everything to do with red fever."

"What's that supposed to mean?"

"When the fever first struck, people were terrified. They're still terrified, especially after the recent surge of cases, but not like they were back then. Back then, the feve was new, and it almost destroyed us. It almost destroyed me." He clenched a fist, his head angling down like he was walking into the wind. "I fought the insanity welling inside me. I fought the horrors that plagued my mind, the urges that told me to kill. I meditated for months. All day, every day. I stuck tubes in my arms to keep me alive, so I wouldn't have to stop for food or water. I learned to control it, Denver. I conquered it, and all I've done since is try to teach others how to defeat it. The fever will ruin us if we let it. Earth is dying. Its moon is a sterile rock. Mars is humanity's only hope, and if we let the feve have its way, we'll be extinct. Your grandfather didn't understand that."

"The hell he didn't. He founded this world with you. You think he didn't want to create a better life for Martians? Ojiisan started Jericho. He was the one who saw the potential in Doctor Werner, and now that he's in charge, he's bringing us closer and closer to being able to walk outside without an enviro-suit."

"A necessary evil, that doctor, and I want to emphasize the evil over the necessary."

"At least he was honest with me. He gave me the data I wanted, and he didn't manipulate it like you did. How could you be so cruel to imprison Ojiisan? He was your best friend. Your partner. You stripped him of who he was and left him out there to suffer."

"He left me no choice, Denver. Death would've been a kindness he didn't deserve."

"For what? What did he do to you that was so awful?"

A monk entered the cabin and shook her head. *He's not here.*

Hennessey turned to me. “Where is he, Denver?”

“Rafe has him.”

His eyebrows lifted. “Rafe Ranchard?”

“The one and the same. He wants back into the church.”

“I suppose he does. If he hands Tatsuo over, perhaps I’ll have to grant him his request.”

“He thinks you manipulated the records that got him excommunicated.”

Hennessey confirmed the accusation with a satisfied grin. To one of his monks he said, “Lock them up for now.”

He walked for the door, his boots clomping loudly on the decking. I stopped him with my voice. “You never answered my question. What did my grandfather do to you that was so awful?”

He turned around and put his hands together in a priestly pose. “It wasn’t what he did to me, child. It was what he did to you.”

And then he was gone.

CHAPTER SEVENTEEN

I SAT ON THE FLOOR INSIDE A CUBE OF ROCK. A single weak bulb hung overhead. The door was locked, and all I could do was wait for Hennessey to decide what he wanted to do with me.

<Smith, can you hear me?>

Again, nothing. I'd been checking every so often for what seemed like hours, but he'd either been powered off or he was out of range.

I didn't know where Navya or Nigel were. I suspected they were being held somewhere in the same cathedral, but I couldn't be sure. They'd done so much for me, I just had to hope we'd all get out of this mess so I'd have the chance to make it up to them.

The snick of the lock brought me out of my seat. The door opened and Hennessey stepped inside. "I have him now."

"Ojiisan?" I asked.

He nodded.

"So you gave Rafe what he wanted?"

"Yes, he'll be reinstated. I know how dangerous he is, but there's something to be said about keeping your enemies close."

I let out a heavy sigh. "Where are Navya and Nigel?"

"They're upstairs. The botsie has been deactivated, and the pilot is sleeping."

"Let them go."

"I'd love nothing more. But they know too much."

"What does that mean? That you're going to kill them?"

"You killed one of mine, remember? Wouldn't that make us even?"

"Your men were trying to kill me! What did you expect? And I only killed one of your men. I've got two friends up there."

"Who would you pick, the pilot or the bot? You already know my position on botsies. I'd be doing this world a favor by permanently shutting him down."

"Go to hell."

"I warned you, Denver, but you wouldn't leave it alone. You just kept sticking your nose where it didn't belong. If you'd succeeded in restoring Tatsuo's memories, Mars would already be lost. I'm sorry, but your lives are worth the sacrifice."

"So you're going to kill us then? All of us?"

"I hope not, child. I really hope not. But I won't lie to you, it may yet come to exactly that. Let's call the current situation fluid. You should've let it go, Denver. You shouldn't have brought them into this."

"Don't give me that shit. You're the one who brought us all into this by stranding my grandfather on the surface. You're the poison pill, not me."

He raised his hands in a placating gesture. "Fair enough, child. But it's your grandfather who poisoned us all, and he's the one who wouldn't accept his punishment. He's the one who left those messages. He's the one who archived his memory for you to find. He wanted you to rescue him and restore his memory so he could rise from the dead."

"Punish him for what? You still haven't told me what he did."

"And I won't."

I'd had about enough of his bullshit. "That's because you're afraid to tell me. It's because you know that whatever he did, he didn't deserve what you did to him. You won't say because you know you're going to sound petty and small. You wanted Mars for yourself, didn't you? That's what this is really about. You were tired of sharing the power and the glory, and you wanted to steal it all for yourself."

His face didn't move as he listened, and it didn't move now that I was done. When he spoke, his voice was calm and steady. "Do you want to see him?"

My eyebrows jumped with surprise. "Of course I do."

Without another word, he stepped out and the door locked behind him.

Too amped to sit, I paced the small area, back and forth, back and forth, my mind racing in a million different directions. Minutes passed, and the door opened again. A monk stood outside, her head bowed in obedience to an unseen power.

She waved, and Ojiisan stepped into view. For the first time since I was a girl, my grandfather, the man who raised me, stood before me.

He was much thinner than I remembered. Thin enough, it seemed a breeze could whisk him away. The skin had begun to sag around his mouth and under his chin. He raised a knobby hand and rubbed his cheek like he was still getting used to being clean shaven. His hair was white, and had been cut close to the scalp.

His eyes, they were exactly how I remembered.

I pulled him forward and wrapped my arms around bony shoulders. "Whatever happens," I said, "it was all worth it." I released the hug and held his face with a hand on each side. "I don't care if they kill us. To have this moment, it was all worth it."

He smiled, but it wasn't the smile of a man reunited with his long-lost granddaughter. His was the polite but uncomfortable smile of a man who didn't know where he was. Or who I was. Or who *he* was.

The door was still open, the monk standing in the hallway. Thinking it odd that the door hadn't been secured, I gave the monk a second look. Her lips were moving like she was subvocalizing, and she kept turning her head to look left then right.

Ojiisan seemed to pick up on my concern and turned around to look at the monk as well.

Her eyes met mine, and she held up a finger, telling me to wait. Then she moved that same finger to her lips. *Stay quiet.*

Could she be an ally? Could she get us out of here? My heart was already pounding in my chest.

I noticed a bump on her hip, a weighty bump under her silk robes. <Smith?>

<I'm here, Denver.>

<Who is she?>

<I don't know, but she stole me from Hennessey's desk and brought me here.>

The monk waved us forward and ushered us to the right. I clasped my grandfather's wrist and led him into the hall. The monk started down the corridor moving fast enough that I had to hustle to catch up before she started up a set of stairs.

"Who are you?" I asked, my voice an urgent whisper.

"Shhh."

"Where are you taking us?"

She turned to me, all of the lines on her face angling downward. "You want to live, then shut up."

"You listen to me, dammit. I'm not taking another step until I know who you are."

Her eyes flashed with annoyance. "Doctor Werner sent me."

"Doctor Werner? Why?"

"You can ask him when you see him."

She made to go up the stairs, but I grabbed her shoulder. "Give me my gun."

"No."

I held out my hand. "The gun. Give it to me."

Ojiisan moved between us and urged me to take step back. "Whoever she is, it seems she wants to help us. Maybe you can do what she says?"

I had to smile. Confused as he must be, he'd seen and heard enough to know how dangerous Hennessey was. Ojiisan's message was clear. . .wherever this was, we'd be better off anyplace else.

"We'll do what you say," I said to the monk. "But I'm not leaving without Navya and Nigel."

The monk nodded. "Fine. They're upstairs."

I followed her up the steps, my grandfather trailing right behind me. We navigated down a hallway, the monk stopping to check every doorway we passed. Approaching a corner, I could hear voices echoing from around the bend. After peeking past the corner's edge, she waved us forward. Hustling past the opening, we arrived at another door, and she palmed the lock open. Inside, Navya sat on the floor.

"Denver! They let you go?" Navya asked.

I shook my head and eyed the monk. "This one's sneaking us out. Don't ask why."

Navya acknowledged with a nod and snapped her fingers. "Then let's get the hell outta here." She jumped up and we moved down the hall to another door. The monk unlocked it and we entered.

Nigel was laid out, looking uncannily like a corpse in his powered off state.

The monk said, "Leave it. We don't have time to carry deadweight."

"No need," Navya said and approached Nigel. She reached a hand for his hip and dropped two fingers inside his belt. After bit of fidgeting, she found what must've been a backup switch, and Nigel came to life.

Navya smirked and pulled her hand back. "Just gotta know how to turn 'em on."

"Well hello, love," Nigel said with a wink and stood, brushing himself off. "What did I miss?"

"No time to discuss," I said. "C'mon, we need to move."

"Aye, mate."

Five of us were now single-filing up another staircase, the scent of incense tickling my nose. At the top, we passed through an arched door carved from rock. Beyond it was the cathedral's main hall. Rows of intricately carved columns reached to a ceiling of stone and glass.

"We're heading up there," said the monk. Up there

was the planet's surface, the closest way out of the underground complex of lies and false prophets.

The great hall was empty except for a few parishioners kneeling in prayer. Quickly, the monk ushered us toward the altar, guiding us through a thick cloud of smoky incense. The woody, herbaceous aroma scratched at the back of my throat. We ducked through a door behind the altar to a set of metal stairs. I looked up. At least a dozen flights of stairs and catwalks crisscrossed their way to the door that would lead us out. We started climbing, the metal stairs shaking and swaying like an Earth-style fire escape. Separating us from the cathedral's giant hall was an impossibly tall wall of stained glass that filtered the dim light into shards.

I took the stairs quick, my eyes darting back and forth to the door above and the stairs below. Nobody coming in either direction. Our escape hadn't yet been detected.

I kept climbing, my grandfather right in front of me. The monk in front of him. Navya and Nigel followed behind me. Cresting one set of stairs, we crossed narrow catwalks to the next set. Up and up and up, we were already halfway.

I looked down at the stone floor shrinking farther and farther away. The thin, iron bars that acted as railings seemed more inadequate the higher we climbed. Glancing at the stone floor again, the vertiginous drop gave my mind a wobble. I looked away, choosing instead to focus on the door above, our exit to safety.

The door opened. I froze, my foot on the top stair of the most recent flight. Sensing I'd stopped, my grandfather stopped too, and so did the monk, both of them standing on a catwalk. From the door high above, a group of eight monks started down the stairs, some carrying pickaxes, others carrying guns.

Their footfalls sent vibrations all the way down the shoddy metalwork until I felt them under my shoes and where I held the guardrail tight in my fist. My eyes turned downward to catch more monks racing up the stairs below.

CHAPTER EIGHTEEN

"I NEED MY GUN." MY VOICE SOUNDED LIKE a growl.

The monk hesitated before tearing her eyes off the group of enemies descending the stairs. Her face was painted with a patchwork of eerie lighting coming through the stained glass. Her lips were moving, subvocalizing into some kind of tech wired in her head.

"Gun," I said. "Now."

She kept moving her lips, her eyes dashing every which way like she was navigating a holographic display only she could see.

"I need my gun, dammit!" I reached around my grandfather, my hand stretching for her hip. I'd throw her overboard if I had to.

She twisted around to block me with her other hip, and she grabbed my wrist, her grip tight enough to make me whelp.

"Let me go!" I hissed.

She shook her head, the light dancing across her features. A bright flash lit in her eyes, a quickly extinguished blaze right behind her irises. I sucked in a breath; what the hell did I just see? It was the same strange flash I'd seen in the doctor's eyes when I met him just a few days ago. The only time I'd seen anything similar was at the Earth Park, when a group of cats' eyes glowed in the beam of a spotlight mounted in their enclosure.

She pointed upward. "Come, we have to hurry."

Looking up, I expected the armed monks to be bearing down on us by now, but they'd stopped their approach.

"What are they doing?" asked Navya.

Nigel climbed the rest of the way up to the catwalk. "The monks down below stopped too."

A shout sounded from one of the monks above. No, not a shout, more of a cry, a long, mournful cry. Then the monk tipped forward and flipped over the rail. Ojiisan and Navya gasped in unison. With a dropped jaw, I watched him fall straight toward us. His white robes flapped and snapped like a flag in high wind as he plummeted like a stone. He sped right past me, close enough to touch, his tortured face zipping by in an instant. He hit a railing below, his arms and legs whipping against a snapped back. The shock vibrated up the stairs to rattle my already shaken nerves.

What the hell was happening?

The body tumbled farther to smack the stone floor with a stomach-turning slap.

The sound of a pulseripper snatched my attention. Above, two more monks toppled to their own gunfire. Stunned, I watched a pickax find its target, the sharp end driving through one side of a monk's skull to jut out the other side before the victim collapsed onto the catwalk.

"Now!" shouted the monk who had led us here. She sprinted halfway up the next set of stairs while the rest of us stood frozen in shock and horror.

Nigel guided me forward. "Come on, love. No time to dawdle."

I gave my grandfather a light push, and we were all on the move again. From behind me, I heard Navya point out what should've been obvious.

"The feve," she said.

CHAPTER NINETEEN

THE FOUR OF US, OJIISAN, NAVYA, NIGEL AND I, were all in Doctor Werner's workshop. Hordes of circuit boards and chips, cogs and hydraulics littered what must've been hundreds of shelves and tables in this warehouse of a room. Throughout the space, unearthly franken-machines built of spare parts sat in various states of completion or disrepair. Nigel was particularly interested in the machines.

Navya and my grandfather both squinted their eyes against the bright ceiling light that still disturbingly flicked on and off over Werner's desk. I sat with them while Nigel wandered the narrow aisles of parts between the dangerously top-heavy shelves like he was browsing a store. The doctor, so we'd been told, would be joining us shortly.

For the last half hour, we hadn't seen the monk who had led us here. On the way, she hadn't answered a single one of our questions. Who was she? Why was she helping us? What happened in that cathedral? Did she really summon red fever on command?

And there was one more question I hadn't yet dared to ask. What was that flash I had seen in her eyes?

<Denver?>

Relieved to hear he was still nearby, I said, <Yes, I'm here. Are you okay? Where are you?>

<The monk still has me. We're in the next room over. Her name is Bow. Bow like a bow and arrow.>

<Who is she? What is she?>

<I don't know, but whoever she is, she's not wearing robes anymore. Considering where we are, I have to assume she worked for Doctor Werner all along. She must've infiltrated the church and worked her way into Hennessey's inner circle. Is Tatsuo still with you?>

<He is.>

<I'm glad,> he said. <So very glad for you and for him. You know, when I was in Hennessey's office, I talked to Thomas.>

<Haven't you learned your lesson? He doesn't care about you. He just wants to manipulate you.>

<I know. I didn't grant him access to any of my systems. We just talked.>

<What about?>

<We talked about me. For all these years, ever since you added your grandfather's memories into my mind, I've wondered who I was. Was I Tatsuo Moon, co-founder of Mars City? Or was I Smith, just your average AI who

happened to be carrying a human's memories? To be honest, one way or the other I would've been content. But then that message popped up. That message your grandfather left twenty years ago. That really bothered me.>

<Why? Without that message, we wouldn't have rescued him. That message was a good thing, Smith.>

<Indeed it was. I won't argue that. What bothered me was the idea of a message being buried deep inside me. Buried so deep I didn't even know it was there. If that message was there, then what else might be lurking inside? What other memories are hidden from me? What else might I do? What else might I be *compelled* to do? It was very disconcerting.>

<*Was* disconcerting? As in it's not disconcerting anymore?>

<I feel much better now, Denver. I feel like I finally found my purpose. I knew it the instant I heard your grandfather speak. I knew it the second it became apparent he had no memory of his life before being imprisoned in that bunker. Somehow, he must've known Hennessey was going to wipe his mind, and he backed up his memories, and he left them in that helmet for you to find. He knew that if he left enough breadcrumbs, one day you'd reunite him and his memory.>

<Yes,> I said. I looked at Ojiisan. His face was quiet. Serene. It was staggering that a man could play such a long game. Twenty years, he'd lived out there on the

surface. Knowing he'd make his return, he'd submitted to twenty excruciating years of loneliness and hardship.

<That's my purpose, Denver. To give those memories back to your grandfather. To make him whole again. That was my purpose from the very beginning. I just didn't know it.>

<I'm happy for you, Smith. I really am.>

<I'm like a time capsule full of buried mementos. Like an old chest hidden under the bed that's full of personal treasures. I'm the keeper of a man's life. That's who I am.>

<No,> I said. <You're so much more than that, old friend.>

Doctor Werner and Bow entered from the far side of the room. We waited as they crossed the broad space, his footsteps sounding short and hurried while hers were long and graceful. As they made their final approach, my grandfather, Navya, and I stood from our chairs. A moment later, Nigel appeared from behind some shelves to join us.

"Come," said the doctor. "We'll be more comfortable over here."

We followed him down a zigzagging footpath between stacked crates to a conference table surrounded by chairs. A perfectly fine place to hold a business meeting if not for the papers strewn all over the table's surface. Some were crumpled and others were stacked. Some were hand-drawn sketches and others were jammed with charts and numbers. We all took seats, and I pushed a few papers back to make a space for my elbows.

"It's good to see you, Tatsuo," said the doctor, his hands resting on the table, dirty fingers laced together.

Ojiisan nodded.

"We want to restore your memories. You'd like that, wouldn't you?"

Again, my grandfather nodded, his eyes drawn to the gun Bow set on the table.

"Your memories are in there," said the doctor. "Your granddaughter has been a diligent caretaker these last two decades. You were always such a clever man, but you really outdid yourself this time, didn't you?"

Ojiisan gave a slight bow of his head before saying, "Sorry, but I don't know what you're talking about."

"I suppose you don't, but you will soon enough. My techs are preparing their equipment right now. It won't be difficult to reintegrate your memories. We can bring you to the lab in about ten minutes."

"No," I said. "Not yet. He's not going anywhere until you tell me what the hell is going on. Why did you rescue us?"

Doctor Werner offered an awkward grin. Yellowed teeth stood perfectly straight between thin, pink lips. I studied his eyes, waiting to see if I saw the same flash I'd seen in this office once before. But this time there was no blinking light. Nor were there any shifting patterns of refracted light like the dim beams coming through the cathedral's stained glass that revealed the flash in Bow's eyes. The more I thought about it, the more I knew I'd seen something important. There was something different about these people, and it wasn't just a trick of my monochromatic eyes.

"Don't just sit there," I said. "Tell me what your stake is. Why did you blow her cover to rescue us? How did the feve kick in at just the right time to save us?"

The doctor's chilly grin faded. "There is much you don't know."

"No kidding. Now how about you tell me."

He took a deep breath and let it out with a disturbing wheeze. "It all began twenty years ago. That was when Tatsuo and I made some important…let's call them agreements."

"What kind of agreements?"

"The kind that resulted in great progress as we prepared this world for human habitation. Jericho at that time was a pathetic mess. I know you were young then, but do you remember how long they said the terraforming project was going to take?"

"Three-hundred-and-eighty years," said Navya.

The doctor nodded. "Quite right, but also completely wrong."

Navya and I waited for him to go on, but he let the statement hang like a riddle awaiting a punchline.

"I don't understand," I said.

"I'm sure you don't. You have to understand how expensive this project is. We could do so much more to Mars City, but we don't because resources have to be redirected to solar panels and land movers and bacteria farms. How do you think people would've reacted if they had been told the truth?"

"What truth?"

"That the Jericho project was going to take seventeen hundred years."

My brows lifted. Looking around the table, I saw the same shocked expressions on Navya and Ojiisan's faces. Even Nigel's lips had parted in stunned silence.

"You must be joking," I said.

"I'm not. Tatsuo and Cole Hennessey knew the truth, as did the scientists they hired. But they changed the numbers to sell it to the public. They lied. People could buy into three-hundred-and-eighty years. None of them would live to see it, but it was comprehensible. Seventeen hundred would've crushed the hopes of everybody who had come here. It would've crushed the hopes of everybody who had yet to come. They would've given up on Mars, and this colony would've eventually died."

"But you changed that?"

He gave a slight nod. "Indeed, I did. Your great-grandchildren will be able to breathe outdoors without aid. All of Mars' scientists were inferior. Incapable of harnessing the power of microbes and lichens that could crack oxygen from water trapped in the soil. They didn't see the energy that could be loosed by stimulating volcanos. But I had a solution."

I raised my hands in surrender. "Yes, we bow to your brilliance, okay? Now let's talk about this agreement you said you had with my grandfather."

"I agreed to terraform this world."

"And he agreed to do what?"

"Apologies, but I promised to keep that a secret. If you want to ask your grandfather after reintegration, that's up to you. I trust his discretion to tell you what he wants. Now are we done?"

"No," I said as I formulated my next question. "Why did you leave him out there all this time? If you and he had this great agreement, why didn't you go rescue him yourself? Why did you let him suffer for twenty years until I went and found him?"

He shrugged his shoulders. "Like everybody else, I thought he was dead. It wasn't until his messages started to appear that I thought any different. Even then, I didn't believe it. Even after you came to ask for the data, I still didn't believe it. I considered the possibility remote, right up until Bow called to report that he was being held prisoner by the church. You deserve a lot of credit, Denver, for seeing this through. Without your single-minded determination, he'd still be out there. Now, let's get Tatsuo to the lab."

"Not yet!" I slapped the table. "And stop trying to rush me. We're not going anywhere until you tell me why Hennessey did it. Why did he wipe Ojiisan's mind and strand him out there?"

Doctor Werner responded with a blank stare.

"Answer me, or we're walking right out of here." I reached for Smith and snatched him from the table. Nobody made a move to stop me.

I stood. "Come on, Ojiisan, we're outta here."

But Ojiisan didn't rise. Instead he took my free hand in his. "I don't know you, but I know you care for me. Please, I've been lost for so long." A tear rolled down his cheek. "Let's do what he says."

CHAPTER TWENTY

WINDOWS STRETCHED FROM WALL TO WALL OF the observation deck. On the other side was the lab, a sprawling space of tanks and underwater life aquariums and technicians in white coats. My grandfather was down there somewhere. Probably inside the datacenter where racks of winking lights stood in rows behind another wall of glass.

"He'll be fine," said Navya from the chair on my left.

Nigel, who sat on my other side, nodded his head. "Quite right, love. You know, I'd enjoy the chance to see this through, but Jard must be furious by now." He stood as if to leave.

I took his hand and pulled him back toward the chair. "It might not be safe."

"Not to worry. Jard can swap my chip into another bot. Nobody will know how to find me."

I gave his hand another tug. "I want you to stay."

"But Jard—"

"Let me take care of Jard. Now sit."

He did.

<You've made a good friend,> said Smith from his proper place on my hip. They'd brought him back to me a half hour ago. The memory transfer was complete, and now they were working on removing Ojiisan's implants before waking him up.

<Yes, I did.>

The door opened behind us, and we all turned to find Doctor Werner entering with Ojiisan. The difference in my grandfather was immediately obvious. His eyes were sharp instead of lost. His chin was high. Gone was the weary castaway, and in its place was the confident co-founder of Mars City.

"We tried to tell him to rest a little longer," said the doctor, "but he refused."

I stood and rushed to greet him. He put one hand on each of my shoulders. "Look at you," he said, his smile warm, his eyes vibrant and practically shining. "You're everything I'd hoped you would be."

I tried to speak, tried to tell him how happy I was to see him, the real *him*, but I couldn't find my voice. Tears were already streaming from my eyes, and my throat was choked with glee.

"Now, now," he said as he embraced me and patted my back just like he used to when I bumped my head or got picked on at school. "The gun," he said, "I need you to erase it."

I tensed in his grasp. “W-what do you mean?” I managed to say.

He pulled out of the embrace and tapped his temple with a finger. “I’m all in here now. Do you still have the helmet I left for you?”

“Y-yes, of course I do.”

“Erase it, too.”

I gave him a confused look.

“Trust me,” he said. “Now, rest up. There are important matters I must discuss with the doctor. I’ll return later.”

He gave me a pat on the cheek, and then he was out the door. I didn’t even get the chance to say the memories weren’t in the helmet anymore.

The doctor followed him out, and I heard the sound of the lock snatching hold. Stunned, I wiped at the tears on my cheeks, and tried to find my wits. What just happened?

“That was quick,” said Navya.

“Bloody right.” Nigel tried the door to verify it had been locked. “I may be an android but even I know that departure was rushed.”

“Give him a break, Nigel. He’s probably still confused. I bet his mind is racing in a million different directions,” Navya said.

<Denver?>

<Yes?>

<Please don’t erase me.>

<Of course not! I know what he said, but he only

wants the memories erased. He doesn't want me to erase *you*. He probably doesn't even know you exist.>

<You can't erase his memories either, Denver. I've had those memories for more than a few years now, and the speed at which I process code and experiences, that's like a million years to a human.>

<But the memories can be separated, right?>

<No, they're too deeply integrated into me. When they copied the memories into Ojiisan, they did their best, but they had to copy big parts of me, too. Our selves are...intertwined.>

I went to the window, my eyes looking down on the lab again. <Don't worry. I won't let anything happen to you.>

The lab's lights brightened, and most of the white coats moved away from their microscopes and molecular assemblers. The doctor appeared, walking side-by-side with my grandfather. They went to a small stage and stepped up to a podium while the terraforming project's scientists gathered to hear whatever they were about to say. Among them, I spotted the man who saved me from being injected with toxin on the elevator. He didn't wear a lab coat like the others, and the bulge under his jacket hip told me he was part of the doctor's security team.

Doctor Werner started to speak. His hands hung limp at his sides, and he kept his head tilted downward like a kid doing his first book report.

I put my ear to the glass, but couldn't hear anything but my own breathing. Dammit, why did they lock us in?

"I wouldn't worry," said Navya, her hand on my shoulder. "Like I said, he must be terribly confused. I know he rushed out, but you can't put much stock in anything he does right now. You have the rest of your lives to catch up."

Ojiisan took the doctor's place. A holographic ship appeared alongside him, and he spun it around to show it off.

"What kind of ship is that?" I asked.

"Deep space," said Navya. "It's an ark. They were popular a couple decades ago."

Yes, I remembered the arks. At least a hundred of them had launched for deep space. All of them full of colonists who thought the best hope for humanity's survival was outside of our solar system. To this point, none had succeeded in finding a new home.

<Smith, can you see that ship's name?>

<Enhancing imagery now.>

The hologram blinked out to be replaced by a map with a spinning Mars at the center. Ojiisan looked on as a bright dot representing the ark traveled outbound, past Jupiter and Saturn only to turn around and come all the way back, where it fell into orbit around Mars.

<It just turned around and came back?>

<Apparently,> said Smith.

<Why?>

<I have no idea, but I've got the name. The ship is called the *Minds of Mars*.>

<Who is it registered to?>

<To you, Denver.>

<What?> My knees wobbled and I pressed both hands against the glass to steady myself.

"Are you okay?" asked Navya. "What is it?"

"Smith is telling me that ship is mine."

<That's right. It was your grandfather's, but you inherited it when he was supposed to have been dead. It's registered to you.>

<How come I never knew about it?>

<It launched two weeks before your grandfather's disappearance, but it went totally silent six months later. Nobody's heard from it since.>

<What happened to the crew?>

<There was no crew. It was empty.>

I sat down. Navya stood close, wanting to make sure I was okay.

I wasn't. Every time I thought I had the key to unlock the mysteries, the key kicked me in the head.

CHAPTER TWENTY-ONE

ANOTHER HOUR PASSED BEFORE THE DOOR opened again. My grandfather came through alone. His smile felt warm and genuine, but I couldn't summon either emotion for myself.

"Why is the door locked?" I wanted to know.

"Just a precaution," said Ojiisan.

"Are we prisoners?"

"If that was the case, you wouldn't have that gun," he pointed at Smith. "Come, let's get something to eat. The kitchen made something special, just for you."

I looked back at Navya and Nigel. "Can they come, too?"

"Of course."

Following my grandfather, we filed out and into the hall. I smelled something baking and instantly recognized the sweet yeasty scent—*lotus buns*. Fond memories of Sunday brunches at Aiwa and Yaozu's flooded my mind. Aiwa was known for making the best dim sum this side of Mars.

Knowing where Aiwa was now, a dark cloud settled around my heart. I needed to tell Ojiisan what had happened to her and her husband, but not now. Now was a time for celebration.

We entered a sparsely populated cafeteria and I saw the buns sitting in a bin under flickering heat lamps. Everyone but Nigel grabbed a plate. Ojiisan took the two largest buns from the bin.

"You used to love these." He smiled and placed one on my plate.

"I really miss those days," I said, and took a bite.

The bun had a slight metallic taste—a sign the ingredients were manufactured—that instantly killed the nostalgia, but I was too hungry to let it go to waste. Aiwa must've been the only person on Mars with a recipe capable of masking the chemical flavor.

We settled at a four-seat table.

"What was that ship you were showing everybody earlier?"

"It's an ark," he said. "I acquired it twenty years ago."

"What's it carrying?"

"A very special payload." His grin was broad and bright. "When I realized what Hennessey was going to do to me, I made a lot of plans. A lot of long-term plans that are about to pay dividends."

"You know," I said, "I've taken a lot of risks to bring you back, and I don't appreciate being kept in the dark."

He nodded and reached a hand over to take mine. "I know this is hard, and please believe me when I tell you how proud I am of you, Denver. The last twenty years were excruciatingly hard on me, and I know they were hard for you, too. Spending the rest of your youth without a parent is something no child should have to overcome, but overcome you did. Still, there are things you don't know about me and Doctor Werner. Things you don't know about that bastard Hennessey, either. I have so much to tell you, and I will, but it will take time to do it right."

"So let's get started."

"I can't. I'm already late for my meeting with the press."

"They've been waiting two decades to hear from you. They can wait a little longer."

"No. I'm in danger and so are you, Denver. Hennessey's assassins would love to take us out. Once I go public with my reemergence, we'll all be much safer. Do you understand?"

I took another bite and considered the question. "Are you going to let us leave?"

"Yes, of course, you're free to go right now. But you should wait until after the story goes live. Hennessey will have no motive to come after any of you once the public learns I'm alive. That's the secret he wants to keep. Now, did you erase my memories from that gun of yours?"

"I'm working on it."

"Get it done." He stood, grabbed his lotus bun and headed out the cafeteria.

"Bollocks," said Nigel. "He doesn't like to say goodbye, does he?"

I looked at Navya, her eyes meeting mine. "You know what we have to do?" she said.

I nodded my head and dropped some credits on the table. "Let's roll."

I was out of my chair, lotus bun in hand, Navya on my heel while Nigel hustled to catch up. "Where are we going?"

CHAPTER TWENTY-TWO

AFTER EXITING THE TERRAFORMING FACILITY, we headed straight for the shuttleport. I told Smith to record my grandfather's interview with the press. I'd watch it when we were airborne.

Navya's shuttle was back in its berth, and we hustled on board. I hadn't even closed the door before Navya was shouting into the radio, seeking clearance to take flight.

I strapped into the co-pilot's seat, and Nigel took his usual station behind me. I sat with my arms crossed tight. Nobody was going to keep me from finding out the truth.

Not even Ojiisan.

I ground my teeth as our shuttle entered the airlock, and I didn't stop after we'd exited. Navya guided us upward, past the storms, past the limits of Mars' developing atmosphere.

<I have the press recording. Are you ready?>

<Patch into the ship's system so you can play it for everybody.>

To afford plenty of visibility for Navya, a holographic display limited itself to projecting upon the windshield's lower right corner. My grandfather was there, sitting across from a reporter I recognized but couldn't name. Her expression was appropriately flummoxed, and her first question perfectly captured what must be the prevailing sentiment among those who were watching. "You're alive. How can this be?"

Ojiisan offered a coy smile and lifted his hands in a shrug. "I was stranded."

"What do you mean you were stranded? Where were you?"

"I was on the surface."

"For twenty years?"

"Yes, it was more than unpleasant, but I managed to survive thanks to training that, thankfully, I didn't forget."

"But you claim to have forgotten everything else?"

"Yes, I suffered major head trauma in the crash."

"Tell us about the crash, Mr. Moon. Why weren't there search parties? Why didn't we know about it?"

"My ship's tracking system malfunctioned. Nobody knew I was out there. When the ship went down, so did my memories. I'm lucky to have even survived. I couldn't remember who I was until my memory came back recently."

"It came back how?"

"I wish I could tell you. One minute it was gone and the next it returned."

Navya shook her head. "That's not true." She refrained from saying it was a lie, which was exactly what it was.

"But we all thought you were killed by a digger?"

"Did they find my body?"

"No, but—"

"It never happened. Or perhaps it was some other poor soul who died that day."

"What compelled you to take a ship on your own so far away without notifying anyone?"

"I went to scout a region to the south. I was prospecting."

"Prospecting?"

"I knew the area was rich in mineral deposits, and I thought it might be a good location for a second city someday. I had an observation shelter prepared in the area months before the crash. Thankfully I went down close enough to the shelter that I happened upon it when looking for help. But that part of my memory is still foggy."

I crossed my arms so tight they hurt. Why was he lying? Why not tell the truth? Why not take down Hennessey?

<Turn it off,> I told Smith.

<But it's not ov—>

<Turn it off!>

The image blinked out. I could feel Navya and Nigel's stares.

"I don't want to watch anymore," I said. "I've had enough of people not telling the truth. How far are we?"

Navya pulled up a 3-D map. A dot lit and began to move on an elliptical orbit. A label read *Minds of Mars*. "This is us," she said, pointing at a second dot and a line representing our path. "We'll intercept in thirty minutes."

"Is there anyone else out there?"

"The only thing I'm showing in the neighborhood is a salvage ship. They're probably requesting that the *Minds* gets declared fair game so they can claim it. They're a few hundred clicks away, but they'll be on that ship like vultures if they get the all clear. You'd be wise to renew your registration."

<Smith? Get it done.>

<It will be expensive.>

<Do it.>

I sat quiet for the next half hour. Doubts continued to creep in. Was I betraying my grandfather? Should I have waited for him to tell me what the hell happened twenty years ago? If I'd stayed where I was, would he be spilling his story right now?

The questions kept coming, but I had to swat them away. I'd had enough of Hennessey's dodges and Doctor Werner's non-answers. And if my grandfather wasn't going to answer my questions either, then he should've known I'd take matters into my own hands. He was the one who raised me in the first place.

I could see the *Minds of Mars* now. Like a shooting star, it raced in the distance out our port side. Navya adjusted the controls to match its speed and the ship seemed to hang in place against the ink of space. Angling toward its path, I watched the ship begin to take form. Like a long piece of bamboo, it stretched an impossible distance. Built of distinct segments, the ark could never make land or its length would break apart like the cars of a train dropped from the sky. In space though, it was an effective craft. Slow and lumbering but effective in that it could journey for centuries while carrying thousands of people in a self-sustaining ecology.

"Where do we dock?" I asked.

"At least one of those segments will have docking clamps. They'll be easy to spot as we get closer."

The radio chimed. Navya checked the display. "We have a call coming from Doctor Werner's complex. Do you want to answer?"

"No," I said. "Ignore it."

She silenced the call, but it wasn't ten seconds before another chime rang through. "It's the church this time."

"Figures," I said. "Don't answer that one either."

Creeping closer, Navya located docking clamps on the ark's second segment and made the proper adjustments to our flight path.

"Will we be able to enter?" I asked.

"It's your ship, right?"

It was. Somehow, some way, this gigantic hulk of a vessel was mine. At least until my grandfather tried to reestablish his rightful ownership. Slowly, we came closer. Blinking lights illuminated a dull and weathered hull. Navya rotated the shuttle so the ark tilted out of view and was underneath us. She monitored the display, her hand on the yoke, ready to take over if the computer failed to match up the couplers from both crafts.

We made contact with a soft bump, and the ship rocked as the docking clamps grabbed hold. I unbuckled swiftly and moved toward the exit.

"Wait," said Navya. "We need to suit up."

"Why?"

"That ship has no humans on board. For all we know, there's no oxygen. It might not be running artificial gravity either."

Annoyed at the delay, I snatched a suit and a helmet. Nigel grabbed one too. Although he didn't have to breathe like the rest of us, he still processed oxygen into energy to save battery life.

Suited, Navya cycled the airlock, and we stepped inside, closing the door behind us. According to the gauges, there was indeed atmosphere on the other side, but the air sampling app wasn't responding. Whether or not it was breathable was a mystery. We waited for the airlock to match the *Minds of Mars'* air pressure, and when the light gave the all-okay, I spun the hatch wheel and opened the door.

Down a ladder I went, my boots thankfully sticking to the rungs. "Grav is on," I said.

I reached a hand to my faceshield and popped it up to test the air. Immediately, I could tell the air was bad. I didn't smell anything foul, but when I sucked in a breath, my lungs still felt empty. I put the faceshield back in place. "Limited oxygen," I said.

We marched to a security door, and I took off one of my gloves to hold my palm up to the lockscreen. Even though I knew this was my ship, I was still surprised to hear the lock click open.

"Bloody hell," said Nigel. "Turns out our little lass is a starship captain."

We moved into a corridor.

"Where to?" asked Nigel.

"The bridge," I said. I went to the closest maintenance panel and pulled up a map of the ship. As expected, the front-most segment was labeled *bridge*. The other segments were all labeled the same way. *Cargo*.

We headed for the bridge. Maybe when we got there, I'd be able to pull up some kind of log that would give me a clue as to what this ship was carrying and why my grandfather had sent it into deep space only to schedule it to come back just in time for his awakening.

Entering the bridge, I got an eerie chill when I saw chairs and consoles all sitting empty. Navya strode to one of the control systems. "You have to authenticate," she said.

Again, I removed a glove and palmed the lock. Navya quickly located the logs and popped them up on a holographic display. She scrolled down, and we watched thousands of system checks fly by. For a solid minute, she scrolled, but there was nothing there except the same repetitive entries.

She tapped into the camera feeds, hundreds of them running inside the cargo holds. She navigated from one cam to the next, but every single view was dark as night. Then she landed on one that wasn't.

I stepped closer, my eyes trying to make out what I was seeing. The image was hazy and dim, like a piece of parchment was strung over the camera lens.

"Can you zoom out?" I wanted to know.

She did. The image was still a blur, but a pair of shadows resembling black pools had become visible. "What is that?" asked Navya.

"I don't know," said Nigel. "Whatever we're looking at, it must be positioned too close to the camera. The lens can't focus."

Curiosity pulled me forward. I reached for the hologram and touched the image with a gloved finger. My hand sank into the strange shadows. "If I didn't know better, I'd say they were...."

I didn't need to finish the sentence. The twin shadows were oblong, and the spacing between them made them look like...*eyes.*

And then they blinked.

CHAPTER TWENTY-THREE

I GASPED AND YANKED MY HAND AWAY FROM the hologram. My heart instantly kicked into overdrive.

"Holy shit," said Navya. "Did that really just happen?"

I couldn't respond, I was breathing so hard, my heart pounding like I'd seen a ghost. Maybe I had.

"Eyes," said Nigel. "They blinked."

I nodded. "We have to check the cargo holds."

I exited the bridge to make the short walk to the closest cargo bay. Reaching into my suit's pocket, I grabbed hold of Smith and held him out front. I stopped by the doors and tried to swallow down my fear. Exchanging glances with Navya and Nigel, they both gave me a quick nod. *Do it.*

I palmed open the lock.

The doors slid apart to expose a cavern of darkness. I moved into the silent murk, my eyes picking up on a distant glow. We turned on our helmet lights and faint shadows took shape.

"Where the hell are we?" Navya's voice was barely a whisper.

<Smith, map the area.>

<I can't. There's some sort of signal blocking me. I'm surprised we're even able to talk.>

I put my glove back on, and as a group we inched forward. My head bumped into something. Startled, I reached up to find a cable. Aiming my helmet light at the thick cord, it was impossible to tell where it came from or where it was going to.

I could hear Navya's breathing coming across the comm, raking in and out just like my own. I stepped on something and looked down to see another cable, this one running through a puddle. I reached down and touched clear liquid. Rubbing it between my gloved fingers, it felt slick like oil. More cables ran across the wet floor like black eels.

Following the gun in my hand, I moved toward the glow. A loud whir spun up from the right, and I instantly felt the hair stand on the back of my neck. Loud clicks sounded above us, and I looked to see shadows move across the ceiling. Instinctively, I dropped to my knees, the gun gripped tight in both hands.

"It okay," said Nigel. "The shadows move in straight lines. Whatever it is, I think it's robotic."

"Those eyes we saw weren't robotic."

"Agreed," he said. "But those sounds we're

hearing now are. The machines must maintain the equipment in here."

Tentatively, I stood straight, and took a step forward. Then another, and another. Whatever glowed up ahead wasn't as far as I'd originally thought, but it sat behind thick plastic curtains. Navya stayed close enough to bump shoulders with me while Nigel kept a more confident distance.

"I could really use a can of protein paste right about now," he said. "It's proven to be an effective weapon for me."

More cables ran across the floor, all of them snaking in the same general direction. The glowing object was straight ahead. Taller than it was wide, it loomed like a teetering boulder. We continued our painstaking approach and pushed our way through the heavy plastic sheeting.

Close as we were, I still couldn't understand what I saw. Cables lifted from the floor to connect with the object towering before us. Some of the cables, I realized, were actually tubes, pulsing with fluids. A sound emanated from the equipment. A gentle bubbling noise that reminded me of an aquarium.

We were just a few feet away now, our lights starting to penetrate through the disorienting reflections. I saw flesh, a sea of flesh; pale, like it had been bleached.

Hands. Feet. Faces. All of them misshapen and pressing against the glass. I felt cold, every inch of my skin bristling like I'd stepped into a meat locker. My eyes stayed open, processing the horror in front of me. Packed in like jarred fish, their arms and legs were tangled and twisted, making it impossible to match limb to torso.

They were human, men and women both, all of them submerged in some kind of slow-bubbling goo. Their eyes were open, all staring into nothingness. Their skin was so pale it was almost translucent, veins and bones and atrophied muscles all faintly visible under the surface.

Navya bent over and scrambled to take off her helmet. She groaned her lotus bun onto the floor. I dropped to my knees and shook my head. Whatever this abomination was, I couldn't look at it anymore.

There had to be hundreds of them inside that…that *tank*. I looked to Navya to make sure she was okay. Nigel was helping her reattach her helmet.

My eyes blurred with tears.

<Are you alright, Denver?>

I didn't respond. I couldn't. From my vantage on the floor I could see another group of cables meandering toward another tank. And another. Gods, how many of them were there?

Remembering the map of the ark we'd called up earlier, a number began to blink brightly in my mind.

Three-hundred-and-sixteen.

That was how many segments were linked together to form this ark. All of them but one marked as *cargo*.

CHAPTER TWENTY-FOUR

I SAT IN THE CAPTAIN'S CHAIR. AFTER ALL, I WAS the owner of this abomination of a ship. Navya sat to my right, and Nigel worked the control panel behind me.

My helmet was on my lap. Navya had restored full oxygen to the entire bridge section of the ship. But it didn't matter; the one thing I couldn't do was breathe easy.

I didn't think it was possible for anything to horrify me more than the grisly scene I'd witnessed trying to rescue Yaozu and Aiwa from the attack of the feve. But, even after seeing all that blood and death, I'd never felt as empty as I did now.

"Why?" asked Navya. "Why?"

I didn't know. I wasn't sure I even wanted to know.

"This is interesting," said Nigel. "This imagery is from twenty years ago. Not long after the ship first left Mars's orbit."

He ran a time lapse of the camera feeds. It started

with tank after tank full of embryos. Moving forward through the years, the footage showed them growing into babies and the tanks becoming more crowded as a result. Ten years in, the tanks were full of children, the limited space causing their small bodies to twist and warp as they grew and pressed into each other. Limbs began to intertwine, and then the cameras thankfully went dark as the ship must've turned off the lights to save power.

My grandfather bought this ship. He stocked it with equipment and an army of top-notch machines. Somehow, he had access to thousands and thousands of embryos and jammed them into tanks to grow into those over-packed masses of adult flesh.

Why?

"A call is coming in," said Navya. "It's Doctor Werner."

"Answer it," I said.

The screen lit. Doctor Werner sat next to my grandfather. "Hello, Denver," said Ojiisan.

"Hello," I said. My voice came out colder than I expected, and I knew right then that my relationship with Ojiisan would never be the same. There was no going back to who we were twenty years ago. After what I'd seen inside the cargo hold, there might be no going back at all. "What did you do?"

"You went into the cargo holds?"

"Of course, I did. What was that in there?"

"Listen, Denver," said Ojiisan with a slight bow of his

head. "I really wish you hadn't gone up there. If you'd just stayed here, I would've explained everything. I just needed some more time."

"Explain it now," I said.

"Come home, and I will."

"No." I shook my head. "Actually, make that a *hell* no. Start talking, or I'll crash this ship."

Navya's head snapped in my direction, and I felt Nigel's hand grasp my shoulder. If they were looking for signs I was bluffing, they wouldn't find any.

Ojiisan scratched his head like he was still trying to figure out what I'd just said.

"Set a course for Olympus Mons," I said to Navya. "Maximum speed. Smash this train into a pancake."

"Aye," said Navya.

I watched the screen, waiting for a response. Doctor Werner leaned toward Ojiisan to whisper something the microphone couldn't pick up.

<Smith, did you see that? What did he say?>

<Doctor Werner has a very flat affect. It makes reading his lips a challenge.>

<Try anyway.>

<I think he said that the subjects were critical to success.>

Subjects? Is that what those people in the tanks were? Subjects for some kind of experiment? An experiment that was twenty years in the making?

Ojiisan cleared his throat. "Denver, I need you to

come home. Leave the ship in orbit and come home so we can hash this out."

"Changing course," said Navya. "ETA sixty-three minutes. I estimate we have thirty-one minutes before gravity grabs hold and there's no turning back."

"You've got a half hour," I said to the screen. "Start talking."

Ojiisan's eyebrows drew close together, and his lips pressed tight. There was a time a look like that would've made me run to my bed. But not anymore. Those were *people* in those tanks. They might be empty shells, but they were still people.

I waited for him to speak. Waited for him to tell me what this grand plan of his was. He'd allowed Hennessey to imprison him on the surface for twenty long years in order to unleash this mad scheme, and whatever the purpose, he was going to tell me or see this ship smashed headfirst into the solar system's largest volcano.

"I did it all for you," he said. "I did it for us, for our future. You don't understand the situation you're putting me in. I planted these seeds so, so long ago, and they're just about to bear fruit."

"Why did you raise all those people in those tanks? Are they brain-dead?"

"Of course not," said the doctor. "What purpose could they possibly serve if that were the case?"

I took the news like a punch to the gut. It was appalling enough to think they were empty vessels, but this newest outrage made my lips and hands tremble. "How could you, Ojiisan? You, of all people, know what it's like to be a prisoner. How can you go forward with this now?"

"Because of you, Denver."

"Don't use me as an excuse. You trapped those people in their own bodies. You tortured them!"

"Denver, please," said Ojiisan. "I beg you to put that ship back in orbit and come home. I'll tell you everything."

I shook my head. I was so sick of being strung along. Maybe it was time to start drawing my own conclusions.

I sat tall in my chair, and pointed a finger at the doctor. "You, you're responsible for all of this. Your assistant, Bow, she was able to command red fever at will. That's what this is all about." The truth slapped me right in the face. "You've been messing with all of our heads, and that's what these people are for. The *Minds of Mars* is full of brains for you to experiment on."

He met my words with a matter-of-fact stare.

"And you, Ojiisan, you built this ship to help him."

"He's terraforming Mars," said Ojiisan. "We couldn't do it on our own. We'd go extinct. Preparing that ship and raising those brains to be lab rats is a small price to pay. Now put that ship back in orbit." He let his voice go quiet for a moment. "Or else."

"Or else what?"

The door to the bridge slid open, and Bow stepped inside, a pulse pistol aimed at my head.

Shit. I raised my hands slow. "Where did you come from?"

"I stowed away on your shuttle. I suspected you might pull something like this. The doctor and your grandfather told me I was being paranoid, but it appears I was right. Your gun. Pull it out slow and drop it on the deck."

"No," I said with as much defiance as I could muster. "My grandfather won't let you shoot me."

She raised an eyebrow. "I don't take orders from your grandfather. Trust me when I tell you I won't hesitate."

"Listen to her," said Ojiisan, his voice sounding genuinely concerned. "Give her the gun, Denver."

Slowly, I reached for my suit's pocket. I took hold of Smith, and, careful to keep the barrel aimed at the floor, I pulled him free.

"Drop it to the deck," said Bow.

Nigel jumped between us. Bow unleashed a pulse that took him in the shoulder. A blast of hydraulic fluid and carbon-fiber shrapnel struck me in the face.

CHAPTER TWENTY-FIVE

VISION BLURRED, I DOVE TO THE DECK, SWING-ing Smith in Bow's general direction.

I didn't need to pull the trigger. Smith fired at just the right time, and a pulse ripped outward. Growing in size as it travelled, it hit her chest and blew her entire body backward to slam against the door.

She crumbled into a heap on the floor.

<I got her, Denver!>

<Nice work.>

I blinked my eyes clear and looked up at Nigel, who wobbled and fell on top of me. Feeling crushed under his weight, I had to scramble to squeeze out from under him. A giant divot had been taken out of his shredded shoulder. Fluids and oils mingled on the floor. Somehow his arm was still attached. His eyes were still open, but fading.

"Bollocks," he said.

Navya had already torn off the arm of her suit, and

she rolled it into a ball and pressed it into the wound. "What were you thinking?" she said.

When he spoke, his voice was slurred. "I thought maybe I could stay with all of you. Maybe Denver could buy me away from Jard."

I stood and leaned into the path of his eyes to make sure he saw me. "You can count on it, my friend."

I turned to the screen. The doctor had stepped away, but my grandfather still sat where I'd last seen him. His face was ashen, but I couldn't be sure if it was because he was worried about me or his precious cargo.

I walked to Bow's body, and kicked the gun away. The angle of her spine told me her back had snapped, but I saw a gentle lift and fall to her chest. She was still breathing. I turned her face upward to look into her eyes.

"Navya, flick the lights," I said.

"What are you talking about?"

"The lights. Turn them off and back on. Do it fast."

She did, and I stared close into Bow's eyes, stared until I saw the bright flash that reminded me of a cat caught in a beam of light. It came just like it had two times before, only this time the iridescence lasted far longer than a moment, long enough that I could see her eyes weren't really like a cat's at all. What had looked like a consistently reflective image in the past was—thanks to the close-up view—actually composed of hundreds of tiny dots.

"Do you see it?" I asked.

Nigel was close enough to Bow to see her face. He craned his neck and then shook his head. "All I see are the eyes of a dying woman, Denver."

"No, there's something else. It happens right as the light catches her iris. I noticed the same thing with Werner."

"I'm sorry, love," he said and rolled onto his back. "Perhaps it's something only humans can see. Navya should have a look."

Navya fiddled with the console until the room's lights strobed and then crouched next to Bow's crumpled body. She stared for a long moment before looking at me.

"Whatever it is you're seeing, Den, I'm not..."

Was I going crazy? Then Smith chimed in.

<You know, Denver, it's possible that you're able to see something none of us can because you're monochromatic.>

I supposed that was possible, but I'd never heard of such a thing before. My disability always meant I was missing things others could see, not the other way around.

Bow coughed, and took what I thought was her last gasp of air. But then she coughed again.

And then she moved one of her legs.

I jumped back.

That wasn't possible. Her other leg moved too, like she was trying to right her impossibly wrenched back.

There could only be one explanation. All those

crackpots and cranks yammering on about aliens were right. It wasn't paranoia. It was the truth. Thoughts dominoed in my mind. Knots untangled. Cobwebs turned to dust and blew away. For the first time since I'd started on this insane journey I felt like I was seeing clearly.

She managed to move a shoulder, but she still had a long way to go to right herself.

I retrieved her gun and went back to my captain's chair. Navya tended to Nigel, who still held a charge.

Navya pointed at the console, and the timer that was steadily ticking downward. "Eleven more minutes before this ship sinks too far in the gravity well to get back out. A half hour later, this ship will impact the volcano. We need to be on the shuttle soon."

"Understood."

I faced my grandfather.

"Denver," he said, "I'm so glad you're okay. But this really has gone on long enough. Put that ship back into a safe orbit and come home before somebody else gets hurt."

"She's an alien," I said.

"What?"

"You heard me. She and the doctor, they're not human."

"You're sounding crazy, Denver. Are you sure you aren't injured?"

I said the words as they came into my head.

"Everybody thinks the doctor is such a genius, but he's not really that smart, they just have technology we don't."

My grandfather watched me, his eyes blinking quickly. The doctor appeared on screen again to stand behind my grandfather.

"You're an alien," I said to him. "I saw something in your eyes, and I saw it in hers, too." I glanced in Bow's direction. She'd made progress getting her arms and legs lined up correctly, but her spine was still twisted at an unnatural angle.

"Your eyes," I said. "They're compound like a bee's. Somehow you manage to disguise them, and the rest of your real body. You pass as human, but you're not."

He tipped his head and rubbed dirty fingers together.

"You're a damn bug," I said.

CHAPTER TWENTY-SIX

THE DOCTOR TURNED TO MY GRANDFATHER, who offered a shrug as if to say she's already got it figured out so you may as well tell her. Then he looked at the camera with newfound charisma.

"On your Earth, I know insects are basic life forms, but it's not like that everywhere. You see how Bow is being repaired? Clearly, we're far more advanced than humans. Even that android of yours is more durable than you."

Something about his choice of words bothered me. "You said she was *being repaired*? Why didn't you say she's *repairing herself*?"

"You're familiar with the concept of drones?" he asked with a sinister grin.

"She's a drone? Like a worker bee? Is she under your control?"

"Not exactly. She is quite advanced and therefore has

some autonomous functions, but she's also submissive to the hive. As am I."

I could barely put voice to my next thought. "Is that what these experiments are all about? You're trying to turn us into worker bees? You want us to be your drones?"

"Yes," said a resigned Ojiisan. "And in exchange, they'll terraform this world so the human race can live on."

I came halfway out of my chair. "As drones? Slaves?"

"Yes, but they need to perfect the process first. Something hidden deep within our minds keeps them out. They've been experimenting for decades, but the human brain is damned complex, and they haven't quite managed to gain control. They keep trying, but all they've done so far is drive people insane. That's what the fever really is: a side effect of a breached mind. But I negotiated a deal that they'd never harm you and me—or any monochromatic—when they figure it out. I protected you, Denver."

Doctor Werner nodded in agreement.

I thought of Aiwa and the other colonists who'd gone mad recently. "The latest outbreak of the feve was targeted at the original colonists, wasn't it? Those were the brains you've had the most practice on."

Doctor Werner nodded. "Yes, we've collected more data on those than any others. We're close to mastering the human mind, but that latest experiment was still a failure."

"They need brains," said Ojiisan. "And I'm giving

them more than they ever imagined. Working their mind control experiments from a distance has slowed them down. And if they abduct test subjects, they'll attract too much attention. So they've been doing everything remotely—and the fever is the result. But when I deliver that ship to them, they'll have real, live brains in their lab, brains they can touch, brains they can open, brains they can attach to their equipment. They'll finally have direct access to the human mind. From there, it won't take them long to perfect their techniques, Denver. The takeover will be complete, and red fever—and all of its violent side effects—will be a thing of the past."

I looked at my friends. Navya stared at the screen, her face numb with shock. Nigel's eyes had begun to swim, and he was struggling to keep them open.

"Their planet is dying too," said Ojiisan. "They came here and offered me a deal. They'll terraform Mars and save the human race. Not all of us have to be drones. All the other conquered worlds were allowed a few hundred who live free."

"We're not monsters," said the doctor.

"How kind of you," I said. Based on the doctor's lack of expression, I wasn't sure if he understood sarcasm.

"Some of us will live free," said Ojiisan. "And I made sure that some of us was you and me, Denver. You see why I exempted monochromatics? We are the future bloodline. Our condition is genetic, so if you decide to have children one day, they will be exempted too. I love you, Denver."

My eyes began to water. "Does Hennessey know?"

"Yes, of course he does. We're the co-founders of Mars City. The aliens came to us both."

"They offered him the same deal?"

"They did. But Hennessey thinks he can fight their mind control with meditation and discipline and spiritual purity. He doesn't get it, Denver. He doesn't realize this is a battle we can't win. Whether it takes one year, or twenty or a hundred, they'll crack the code to the human mind. They've conquered dozens of races, most of them a hell of a lot more sophisticated than us. So I took the deal. I took it despite Hennessey's objection. People might be enslaved, but humanity will survive, and not all of us will be drones. You and I, and dozens of other monochromatics, will be allowed to flourish here. And when Mars becomes habitable, our population will grow. And in two thousand years, when Earth is no longer toxic, we'll settle it too."

I sank into my chair, and wiped the tears from my cheeks. Finally, I had the answers I'd been seeking, but I felt no relief for the knots wringing my stomach. "Hennessey thinks you're a traitor. That's why he imprisoned you on the surface."

"Yes, for agreeing to the deal. Even then, he was already the most powerful man on Mars by a longshot. If he wanted to cast me out to the surface, I knew I couldn't stop him. It was Aiwa who helped me. She and Yaozu somehow got wind of what he was planning to do to me."

"Yaozu and Aiwa knew about the aliens?"

"No. Nobody knows about the aliens except for Hennessey and me. For everybody else, the aliens are the subject of paranoid fantasies and conspiracy theories."

"You know Yaozu's dead. And Aiwa is institutionalized. Both were victims of the doctor's most recent experiment."

He nodded, and I could see real pain in his eyes. "I know, Denver. But what does it matter? What do any of us matter when we're talking about the extinction of the human race?"

I rubbed at the headache straddling my eyes, my fingers coming away black with oil. "Why didn't Hennessey kill you instead of stranding you on the surface?"

"Thinking back on the last twenty years, a part of me wishes he had. He told me killing me was too light a punishment. He wanted me to suffer, and he figured that even if I did get rescued one day, I wouldn't have any memory of the deal I'd made. Twenty years of solitude. Twenty years of hope turned to despair each and every time one of those drop ships appeared only to turn and leave. It wasn't being alone that made it unbearable, Denver. It was the games. He made sure I knew someone was toying with me."

Slowly, I nodded my head as the last piece of the puzzle clicked into place.

"Why did you lie to that reporter?" I asked. "Why didn't you tell the press what he did to you?"

"Tell them *what* he did, and I'd have to tell them *why* he did it. So that snake gets a pass for now. But don't you doubt that I aim to settle the score one day. I committed treason against humanity? Me? I'm the one who is about to *save* humanity. Without the aliens, we would've failed to terraform Mars. The time estimates were even worse than the doctor told you. We would've lost hope. Eventually, we would've reassigned the resources spent terraforming on some other project. Our death would've been slow, but our death was inevitable."

"What about the arks?"

"The arks are doomed to fail. There aren't many habitable planets nearby, and those that are, are already controlled by the aliens. Hennessey was blinded against all reason. Back then he was just starting that church of his, and he sicced his followers on me, but thanks to Yaozu and Aiwa, I managed to evade capture for a short while. That was when I commissioned this ship. That was when I downloaded my memories to that helmet. I knew, with your help, I could come back in twenty years and honor the deal I made with the aliens and save us all."

"How did you know they wouldn't have already taken over our minds?"

"I didn't. But if they had, they'd have no use for me, and no reason to keep the monochromatic exemption. And if that was the way it turned out, my little comeback would've been a failure. But I also knew they'd failed to crack our minds so far, and if they were still struggling two decades later, I was going to be prepared to offer a sweetener to get our deal back on track. So I commissioned that ship, and I jammed the thing full of as many brains as it could store. And now those brains are fully matured and ready for exploitation."

He clenched his fist. "Mars is ours, Denver. All you have to do is join me, and we can take it."

I slumped even farther into my chair. The truth had finally been laid bare, and all I wanted was to bury it so deep I'd never have to face it again.

"Put the ship back in orbit, Denver."

"If Hennessey knew about the aliens all along, how come he hasn't locked them up and executed them?"

"They're shapeshifters. They're among us. Nobody knows who they are."

"He knows who Doctor Werner is."

"Yes, but the doctor is terraforming this world. Hennessey is terrified they will master their mind control, but he also knows he can't terraform this planet himself. It's a race, see? Hennessey hopes he can use his religious discipline and meditation to thwart the feve once and for all, while the aliens aim to turn us into drones. It's a winner-take-all-battle, and in the meantime, Hennessey allows Mars to continue to be terraformed."

"Four minutes!" called Navya. "I'm transferring ship controls to my shuttle. We need to get moving."

Again, my grandfather repeated his refrain. "Put the ship back in orbit, Denver."

I didn't respond. I was done talking. Done with this entire mess. I was just plain done.

Rising to join Navya, we helped a semi-conscious Nigel to his feet.

"Denver!" shouted Ojiisan. "Put that ship back in orbit!"

"What do you want to do about her?" asked Navya, her eyes aimed at the contorting alien on the floor.

Much as I wanted to leave her, I knew that wasn't my way. "Can you hold Nigel on your own for a minute?"

Navya nodded.

I made quick work of dragging Bow across the room. I opened a hatch in the floor labeled *escape pod* and dropped her through. I didn't make any effort to do it gently. I figured she could self-repair any damage that came as a result. I sealed the hatch and raced back to Navya. "The ship will detect her presence in the pod, won't it?"

"Yes, it should auto-eject before it hits the volcano."

Navya opened the door, and we pulled Nigel through. I didn't bother to look at the screen on the way out. My grandfather was right: Hennessey was a snake, but at least he had the courage to fight the aliens. He'd rallied thousands to his cause, and he was teaching them to fight too. Ojiisan might've been correct that throwing in with the aliens to become a bunch of mindless drones was humanity's best and only chance to survive. But what would be the point? We'd be better off dead.

Hustling aboard Navya's shuttle, I made quick work of getting Nigel started on recharging. He'd need serious repairs, but hopefully a shot of energy would keep him going for a while so I wouldn't have to pull his chip.

The ship shook, and I wobbled my way to my seat. "We undocked?"

"No," said Navya. "Not yet. What the hell?"

"What is it?"

"The *Minds*, it's changing course, moving itself back into orbit."

"I thought you transferred ship control to the shuttle."

"I did." She turned to me, her face white as a sheet. "But we've been locked out."

CHAPTER TWENTY-SEVEN

"WHAT DO YOU MEAN WE'RE LOCKED OUT? That's *my* ship!"

"I don't know what to say, Denver. It won't let me in," Nayva said.

"Move aside." I put my face in front of the facial recognition system.

The system responded with a single word. *Denied.*

"Tell me the course change won't matter." I said. "Tell me the ship is already too deep into the gravity well to turn back."

She shook her head. "It changed course just in time. It'll be a struggle for those old engines, but it will pull itself out."

I squeezed my armrests. "Son of a bitch."

The radio squawked.

"A call's coming in. It's from Werner again."

"Answer it."

Two holograms appeared. One for the doctor and one for my grandfather.

"What did you do?" I shouted.

Ojiisan said, "I filed for ownership of the ship. It is mine, after all."

"But—"

"The fact that you inherited the ship was clearly a mistake since I'm still alive. Normally such a claim takes a few days to process, but the doctor called in a couple favors. It's over, Denver. The *Minds of Mars* will be delivered as expected, and it's time for you to accept reality."

I tapped Navya's shoulder and made a cut-the-connection gesture with my hand.

The holograms disappeared.

I wanted to go through the airlock and try to palm my way inside, but I knew it wouldn't work. I'd been locked out, and there was no way I'd ever get back on board.

"Dammit." I stomped with my boot and pain flared from my heel. "*Dammit!*"

"That's it," said Navya. "We lost."

She was right. As much as I fought against it, there it was, crashing over me like a giant wave. Other than my throbbing foot, I felt completely numb inside.

I raced through my options, knowing none of them could stop what was now inevitable. All I'd wanted to do was save my grandfather, but instead, I'd condemned the tortured souls on that ship to whatever horrors awaited in the doctor's lab. I'd condemned the entire human race to mind control and slavery.

If I'd just ignored that message he left for me, Mars would continue as it had the last twenty years. If I hadn't rescued him, we would limp forward into the future. Broken and damaged compared to the golden era on Earth, but at least we would be free.

But Ojiisan knew me better than that. He raised me. He knew how doggedly determined I could be. He knew how I'd latch onto a thread and wouldn't stop pulling until the entire blanket was unraveled. He knew I couldn't ignore that damn message he left for me. All he had to do was toss me a clue, and he knew I'd be too stubborn to let it go.

<Denver?>

He used me. I was just another pawn on his chessboard.

<Denver?>

And now the entire human race would pay the price.

<Denver?>

<*What?*> I snapped.

<You know the *Minds of Mars* has been in deep space for the last twenty years.>

<Of course I know.>

<Which means its systems haven't been updated in a long time.>

I sat up in my chair, my fingertips tingling with hope. <Can you hack in?>

<No, I don't think so, but I know who can.>

Navya was staring at me. Seeing the sudden hope in my face, she'd perked up as well. "What is it?"

"Call the Church of Mars. I need to talk to the Peerless Leader himself."

CHAPTER TWENTY-EIGHT

"THOMAS HAS BREACHED THE LAST DEFENSE," said Hennessey. "He is in control of the ship now."

I felt the shuttle rock as the massive ship we were still attached to changed course once again.

Hennessey allowed himself a small smile. "You've done well, child. Hold this course for two more minutes, and gravity will doom that ship no matter what your grandfather does."

I nodded my head, tired of talking.

"You remember what I told you?" he asked. "I didn't imprison him because of what he did to me. I did it because of what he did to you."

Again, I nodded. I hadn't understood the first time he'd said those words to me. But I did now. As much as I wanted to believe my grandfather truly wanted to save the human race, I knew it wasn't true. Not entirely.

I'd seen his face when he tried to convince me the world was ours. I'd seen the way he clenched his fist. I'd seen the greed in his eyes. He and Hennessey were the co-founders of Mars City, but on some level, my grandfather knew Hennessey was the stronger leader. He'd seen how Hennessey's church had begun to grow, and how more and more people looked to Hennessey for direction and guidance. Ojiisan knew that as Mars grew, his role would continue to shrink. Already marginalized, he must've allowed his bitterness to color his decision when he made the deal with the alien doctor.

It wasn't what he did to Hennessey that deserved such harsh punishment. It wasn't even what he did to me. It was what he did to us all.

I knew I'd lost the Ojiisan I loved when I was a child—the caring, nurturing man who would go to the ends of the universe to protect me. But the truth was, I hadn't really. He was always with me.

<Smith,> I said.

<Yes, Denver?>

<I'm glad you're here. I want you to know that.>

<I know, Den. I love you, too.>

CHAPTER TWENTY-NINE

NAVYA AND I STOOD ON A SPRAWLING SLANT OF rock just below the crater atop Olympus Mons. At an altitude of more than twenty kilometers, we had perfect visibility. Looking down the slope of the mountain, its rocky surface banked steadily downward, mile after mile, until it disappeared below a boiling skirt of sandstorms.

I looked over my shoulder at the shuttle resting on a mostly flat surface behind us. Nigel had taken my seat. He was still in need of days' worth of repairs, but his condition had improved a bit since getting a fresh charge. "Any second now, love," he said through the radio speaker in my helmet.

<Smith, let me see it in color.>

<Colorizing now.>

Navya's hand lifted to point at the crimson sky.

Silently, a long train of a ship sailed into view. Racing across the sky like a spear, we knew it would impact about six and a half kilometers down the mountainside from where we stood. For a second it seemed to be coming straight at us, but the closer it approached, the more the ship seemed to sink into the atmosphere. Like a bird diving into the ocean, it dropped with reckless precision.

The ship struck, one section piling into the next until a cloud of red dust and rock puffed outward from the side of the volcano like a plume of cinnamon. More than three hundred sections long, the back end of the ship disappeared one section at a time as each was swallowed by the unmovable mass of Olympus Mons. The eerie echoes of heavy breathing inside my helmet were drowned out by the screeching roar of tearing and compacting steel. Vibrations jingled in the stone under my feet, and then it was done.

"What now?" asked Navya.

I let out a long sigh. Destroying that ship was no doubt a victory, but all we'd done was restore the balance of power. The doctor and the other shapeshifters wouldn't stop trying to gain control of our minds. Hennessey and his church wouldn't stop trying to impose their own form of mind control.

And Tatsuo wouldn't stop trying to exploit the situation for his own gain.

"Let's go home," I said as I turned for the shuttle. "The fight continues."

DENVER MOON
METAMORPHOSIS

A SHORT STORY PREQUEL

WARREN HAMMOND & JOSHUA VIOLA

ON EARTH, IT WOULDN'T HAVE BEEN MURDER. On Earth, it wouldn't even have been a crime.

But this was Mars, and robocide was a serious felony. Not as serious as blacklighting a flesh-and-blood human, but prison was prison. Didn't matter if you went in for a dozen or a full fifty, there was no way you were coming out the same.

I pulled my bleached-white hair back into a ponytail and leaned over the bed to get a good look at the so-called victim. Plasteel rods instead of bones. Plastic tubes instead of veins. Plasma-gel instead of blood.

Legally speaking, robocide might be murder, but as far as I was concerned, this spread of human-like body parts was more *like* than *human*. Bots were things, no more than that. You could damage or destroy them, but you couldn't kill them. Bots could be shut down, and that was all.

This one had been shut down pretty good: Her legs were chopped off and tossed aside like toys. Her right arm was scorched and still reeked of burnt plastic. The left arm was missing altogether. Same for her left eye, which had been carved free from a damaged eye socket.

The rest of her appeared to be intact; a prostitute bot stripped naked and ready for action.

My eyes lingered on her lips. No doubt, she was the kind of pretty that could snag a john from across a packed room. The kind of pretty a natural like me could never match.

Pretty just like the other three vics. All hacked to pieces. All missing body parts. The first missing a hand, a foot, and the nose. The second missing the breasts and right ear. The third, the legs, hips and vagina.

All done in the middle of the night. All done with no witnesses. Even the room looked the same. One of thousands of rent-by-the-hour burrows dug into the rock deep below Mars City.

Steel supports flanked a vid screen. A floor lamp stood in the corner. A small pile of credits sat on a bed stand dirtied with dust and flakes the stone walls were always shedding.

"That's four now," Jard Calder said from the doorway behind me. "One every three days."

"I can count," I said.

"Yeah, well, then you can count the days since I called you in. Days you've been drawing pay with no results."

"Thing is," I said, turning around to face him, "results have a bad habit of setting their own schedule."

"And I've got mine." He aimed a thumb at his chest. "Mine depends on keeping my customers happy."

At least he hadn't said *clients*. "And keeping your customers happy depends on keeping your bots working."

"Don't need to be a detective to figure that out, Denver. I know you think I'm loaded, but you gotta understand a business like mine has expenses. Big expenses. New botsies don't come cheap, and neither do repair jobs. I take too many more hits like this and it's all going to crater. My business folds, and you don't get paid. Get it?"

I stepped up to him, close enough to smell Earth liquor on his breath. Business couldn't be too bad if he was importing the good stuff. "You want to call it quits, call it quits. And how's this: I'll drop the case right now and only charge you through yesterday." I pointed an accusing finger. "You think you'd get better results with someone else, then hire another eye."

Jard stared at me long and hard. I stared right back, waiting for him to realize how limited his options were. Ministry officers in this sector were too overworked and underpaid to do a proper investigation. Eyes were common enough, but few carried an artificial intelligence. Even fewer carried my reputation.

Finally, he shrugged and sighed.

"Thought so," I said. "Now how about you tell me something useful. Did you check for her chip?"

"I did, and it's gone. Yanked just like the others."

I moved back to the bed, this time to the opposite

side to observe the carnage from another angle. Leaning close, I studied the synthetic skin around her wounds. Torn, not sliced.

I subvocalized to the artificial intelligence I carried on my belt. <You see that, Smith?>

<I see.> His voice relayed through an implant at the base of my brain. <But it would look a lot better in color.>

<Can't help you there.> I was a monochromatic, and since he was currently looking through my eyes, his view of the world was nothing but gray.

<The tearing around the wounds indicates the murder weapon was dull,> said Smith. <Enhancing imagery now. Give me a few.>

"Think it was the feve?" asked Jard, who was still standing in the doorway.

Couldn't say for sure, but the feve likely played a part. Red fever was bad down here. It was bad everywhere, but the slums where Jard's botsies worked the tunnels were the worst.

Nobody knew what caused it. Or even what it was. A virus? An infection? A parasite? All they knew was that people got it from Mars. Like Mars itself was contagious.

Red fever drove people mad. The kind of mad that made a person massacre a marriage ceremony, or blow up a baby farm. The kind of mad that made a person eat a gun. Or their young.

Many thought it was the red that caused it. Everything on Mars was red. Red rock and sand as far as the eye could see. Even way down here, under the surface, you couldn't escape it. Paint the walls any color you liked, and they'd soon be covered in a dusty, red film. A symptom of the terraforming project that fouled the air supply.

Red fever got to everyone but us monochromatics. If you couldn't see the red, the red couldn't see you. Or so they said. Whether it really was the red that caused the feve was anybody's guess. Color-blocking retina lenses and syntheyes only offered temporary relief. Once you got it, you had it.

"Well?" Jard shifted from one foot to the other. "Is it the feve or not?"

I shrugged. Social skills weren't one of my strong points.

"You think they're selling the parts?" Jard was apparently oblivious to my less than subtle hints I wasn't in the mood to chat.

I shook my head. He was asking the wrong questions. If selling parts was the goal, then why leave so many behind? No two stolen parts were the same. It was like somebody was trying to assemble a new bot. But that, too, seemed unlikely. It was a helluva lot easier to just buy a whole one.

Jard stood still for a moment longer, staring at the remains. Finally giving up on the small talk, he stepped out into the hall and pulled up a laundry cart. "You done here or what? I want to get what's left of her back to my techs to see if there's anything they can salvage."

<Smith, do you have everything we need?>

<Scan complete,> he said. <And I have news for you once that ass gets his bot and moves on.>

<That ass is paying my bills.>

<He's a botstringer, Den. You shouldn't be doing business with a man like that.>

I had to restrain myself from rolling my eyes. Smith's personality was patterned after Ojiisan's, my grandfather, and my grandfather didn't approve of prostitution. Or my line of work.

Jard still waited, one hand resting on the laundry cart.

"Go ahead and get her fixed up," I said.

"She won't be the same, Denver. The customers'll know. There were quite a few...she was their favorite."

"You want to give me their names?"

"You know better than that."

"You're the boss, but you know you're asking me to work this case with one hand tied behind my back."

"At least you've still got both your hands." Jard's voice was thick, like he had emotion for this thing splayed out on the bed.

He pulled the cart through the door. Without facing me, he said, "Find out who did this, Denver. Find out who murdered her."

"I will."

Jard approached the machine.

I wondered what he would think if I called it a machine to his face. If I told him I didn't think it was murder because I didn't think a machine *could* be murdered.

But I hadn't said any of that and never would. I didn't have to agree with Jard, any more than with anybody who hired me. Not as long as they were paying me. Not as long as they were *clients.*

He lifted her torso and gently placed it into the cart. Then he hefted the legs one at a time and tenderly laid them on top.

Smith waited until Jard pushed the cart out the door and disappeared down the corridor before speaking into my mind. <Denver, I told you I found something.>

<Spit it out.>

<When I analyzed the scans of the remains, I found sand crystals in the wound where her arm used to be. Sand crystals like those found in the mines.>

Like those found on a mining tool? Maybe the chisel side of a pickax? <What kind of sand?> I asked.

<Color profile indicates green. Probably olivine.>

<And which mines are rich in olivine?>

<Only one.>

I smiled. Game on.

I'd spent a lot of time working Red Tunnel. It didn't take long to get used to the botsie parlors and porn shops. Same for the human hooktrade. Men and women and combos, straight hetero, all flavors of gay, not to mention trans. Something for every taste, whether the taste ran to flesh-wrapped pay-for-pleasure or synthskin-wrapped pay-for-same.

Keeping to the tunnel's center, I traced a path between two sets of steel rails used to move diggers through the main artery under Mars City. I passed the dark mouths of more tunnels to my left and right that branched off into maze-like warrens.

I paid little heed to the disfigured miners begging for credits. Same for the flashing neon signs outside murder-sim houses where the fevered could get their violence on.

All the vices and indulgences, real and virtual, were represented in Red Tunnel: classic chance games with cards and dice and spinning wheels, liquor bars, pronoid zones, cutmeshops, debasement walkdowns, animallove farms, and pharmapits.

I navigated my way toward Blevin's Mine, the one mine Smith identified as being rich in olivine. I'd never been inside that particular mine, but this neighborhood was still plenty familiar.

I approached a corner bar near the mine where botsies regularly worked the clientele. The place was dead. Being down four bots must've hurt Jard's biz.

I'd spent plenty of nights in that bar working for a number of clients who wanted to get the goods on their spouses. Grabbing admissible evidence of broken vows made up a chunk of my income; some months, the biggest chunk by a good measure.

It occurred to me more than once that the person I was looking for might prefer to take her—or his—revenge in a more physical way, like chopping up the things that led their significant other astray.

Couldn't say I hadn't had such thoughts a year or so back. The memories came quick and strong as I stood here outside this bar, staring at the booth in the back corner, the booth where Connor and I used to sit. I wondered if he was in one of the botsie alcoves right now. I wondered if I still cared, and if I did, I wondered why.

Mostly, though, I wondered if a person in a similar situation could get enough of a rage-on to chop a botsie apart, and then do it again, and twice more after that.

I couldn't rule it out, but like every other theory I'd come up with, it didn't make a whole lot of sense. Somebody juiced or jacked or just plain raged enough to do what was being done to Jard's bots might be just as likely to do the same to the human who'd done them wrong. But there was plenty of wiggle-room in what might be, so I kept an open mind and held that possibility near the top of my list.

I left the bar behind and crossed the street. A bald man in dirty robes stood on a crate holding a sign for the Church of Mars. Shaved from head to toe and branded with a white circle in the middle of their foreheads, the CoMers tirelessly worked the tunnels, their voices constantly spewing the usual ravings about God and sin, and how succumbing to the will of God was the only cure for the feve. Step one, they said, was painting Red Tunnel white. Then work out from there, cleaning up Mars one vice at a time.

They say that back on Earth, half a millennium ago, a crowd of zealots, drunk on religion and high on piety, left one continent and sailed to another just to spread their gospel. Couldn't say the same for those who made the journey from Earth to Mars. We might have a few Christies and Menorahlighters, but Mars wasn't exactly a religious pilgrim's paradise. No, the zealotry that took root here and festered so dramatically was homegrown.

I turned into an alley, the echoing sound of the CoMer's proselytizing following me a long while like the stink of the methane pits. About a third of the population of Mars had joined the church, which meant close to a quarter million people, most of them hating the sex trade bots and everything they stood for. Count the whole lot of them near the top of my not-so-short list, too.

The alleyway opened into a cavernous plaza. To my left was a row of staircases leading to the lower levels. To my right, a bar with nude botsies dancing in the windows. Straight ahead was a two-story structure built of stone blocks braced by aluminum beams. Next to the building stood a pair of gigantic steel doors nearly stretching to the tunnel ceiling, the hinges partially obscuring gears the size of a bulldozer.

Blevin's Mine.

I strode to the building's entrance and let myself in.

Stepping to an unoccupied workstation, I saw a greeting monitor bearing a *Help* icon. I tapped the screen and heard the whir of cameras turning to soak in all five and a half feet of me.

A man's voice came from an unseen speaker. "Can I help you?"

"I need to see whoever's in charge."

"Concerning?"

"Ministry business," I lied.

"You don't look like a ministry officer."

Before I could respond, another voice, this one deeper, broke in. "Door's to your right."

I stepped to the door, and the click of a lock welcomed me through. Dim chemical lights illuminated a rickety stairway. A man waited at the top. He wore a clean set of work overalls, his face crowded by bushy brows and a beard. To my eyes, his hair was the same shade of gray you'd find in a dirty ashtray. There was a circular scar in the middle of his forehead like a CoMer tattoo, only his looked like it'd been scrubbed away with a plasma tool.

"This way," he said, and led me up a steep corridor.

I followed, my mind snagging on that voice. So low it was almost a growl. <Smith, where have I heard that voice before?>

<I don't know. I've only been riding your hip for a few years. Maybe you knew him before?>

The corridor exited onto an observation platform sitting at the mouth of a gaping tunnel that ran outward in a straight line until it tapered into a tiny dot of light. Above and to my right hung the massive gears I spied from outside. A large window behind me looked out onto a plaza filling with miners.

"I like to stand out here during shift changes," the man said. "Good for the troops to see me every day."

"You in charge?"

"Just the super. So tell me, what brings the great Denver Moon here?"

"You have me at a disadvantage." I was surprised he knew my name. "Who exactly are you?"

"You don't remember me?"

It came to me in a flash. The last time I'd seen him, he'd been bald and smooth-faced. "Rafe Ranchard?"

"In the flesh."

Nailing his identity should've made me feel better. But it didn't. My nerves jangled and I tried to convince myself all was okay. Maybe he wasn't the type to hold a grudge.

<Scan him,> I said to Smith.

<Best I can tell he's unarmed. Pupils look good.>

Dilated pupils meant the feve was about to blow. Not a foolproof system by any means, but I told myself to relax just the same. He'd landed on his feet after all. A mining supervisor wasn't a bad job.

Below us, miners came off their shifts and marched to the mess hall. Arriving from elevators or trucks, a small crowd began to file in under the platform.

"So why are you here, Denver?"

I turned to face Rafe, unsure how to proceed. Botsies were a sensitive subject with this guy.

Until I came along, he was high in the Church of Mars, all dignity and commitment to ridding Mars of the scourges of whatever sin was in the sights of his sermon. And his sights were most often trained on the botsies, their customers, and the 'stringers who ran them.

For him, the botsie trade carried an extra measure of vileness because of the sin's true victims.

Botsies.

Ranchard even went so far as to argue that botsies were people. And these people were helpless victims programmed into parlors that imprisoned them for the pleasures of others. He called, with increasing vehemence, for the liberation of the botsies. He wanted them freed, and, once removed from the parlors, given the opportunity to choose the work they desired.

Like a botsie could ever *choose* anything.

"One of your miners is murdering botsies," I said with extra emphasis on the word *murder*. Let him think I saw bots in the same way he did. Maybe he'd actually see past our history and help me. "Whoever it is cuts them into pieces."

He was silent for a time, and my eyes gauged his reaction and then drifted to the miners on the floor below. The crowd began to thin, and I noticed two men in the back, one wearing a hooded jacket over his jumpsuit.

When the hooded miner spotted me taking interest, he grabbed the other by the arm and pulled him in a different direction, away from the observation platform and toward another exit.

<See them?> asked Smith. <Think they're avoiding you?>

"You've got some balls," said Rafe. "After what you did to me, you think I'm going to help you?"

I wasn't going to argue, especially since I'd already found what I came for. "Sorry to bother you, then," I said absently as I turned to look out the window. I stepped to the glass, close enough to fog it, my eyes searching for the two miners avoiding me.

"'Sorry,'" said Rafe. "I like the way that sounds coming out of your mouth. How about you tell me again."

For fear of losing them, I kept my eyes on the window and repeated myself. "I'm really sorry to bother you, Rafe."

There they were, walking fast against the crowd. One peeked back for just a second and then picked up speed.

I had to get out there to track them. I moved toward the exit but bumped into Rafe.

"Sorry," I said again before realizing it wasn't Rafe. I turned around and my stomach tensed. A group of six miners joined us on the platform. Four men and two women with eyes wide and black, all carrying pickaxes.

Rafe grinned. "Now how about you say you're sorry for what you did to me five years ago?"

I glanced out the window once more, just in time to see the pair of miners disappear down one of the staircases that led to the lower levels.

Heart pounding, I backed away from the group to gain some distance but didn't make it more than a few steps before bumping against the railing of the observation platform.

I looked at Rafe, my eyes zeroed on his pupils. "If you're upset, you should take it up with the people who hired me."

Rafe relieved one of the miners of his pickax. "The church thought I was getting too powerful. They told me my message wasn't disciplined or properly grounded in church doctrine."

"Exactly. They hired me to check into your funds. All I did was report the irregularities. They were the ones who shunned and excommunicated you. You want to get revenge, take it up with them."

"They aren't here," he said as he stroked the pickax's handle. "But you are."

His pupils expanded toward the edge of his irises, and I knew time was running out. My hand crept toward the holster on my belt. I was a quick draw, and an even quicker shot, but no matter how quick, one on seven wasn't good odds.

Rafe saw my hand. "Don't even think about it," he said as he hefted the pickax high. He ordered one of the miners to take my gun.

The miner came forward. “What is that thing?” she asked. “An Earth shooter?”

“Smith & Wesson,” I said.

She reached for the handle, and then I heard the sizzle of fried flesh and a scream. The miner reeled backwards, her hand smoking. I grabbed the railing and swung my legs over.

I hit the floor and rolled. Rafe yelled to block the exits, so I ran the opposite way. Deeper into the mine.

<I burned her good,> said Smith.

I would’ve thanked him and told him how happy I was I’d installed him inside the Smith & Wesson, but this wasn’t the time.

<The elevators are your best bet,> said Smith.

At a full sprint, I veered toward the closest elevator, the doors opening automatically at my approach. I rushed inside and slammed into the back wall.

“Close!” I shouted at the voice system. I pulled Smith from his holster, still warm to the touch, and aimed toward the sound of boots clopping my way. Smith went into cannon mode, the Smith & Wesson’s shape transforming into a weapon three times its normal size.

<Go to stun. I don’t need the ministry on my ass over some dead miners,> I said.

<Roger that.>

The doors snicked shut before I could fire.

<Level sixty-three,> said Smith.

I repeated the words for the voice system and the elevator started to plummet. <Where are you taking me?>

<When you get off the elevator, go left, and I'll lead you to an access tunnel that goes to Boxer's.>

Boxer's was the biggest mine on Mars. They'd have a guard shack at the end of that access tunnel. Make it to the guard shack and I was home free.

I waited for the doors to open, sucking air to get ready for the next sprint. I held Smith firm in my right hand, knowing if I couldn't outrun them, I'd have to stun as many as I could. The elevator stopped with a lurch, and the doors finally swished open.

I made it one, two, three steps before hearing the doors of the adjacent elevator.

I didn't look back. Instead, I kept my legs churning, my fists pumping, Smith bobbing up and down in my right hand. Ceiling lights ticked past. I dodged old equipment piled about, sluices and conveyors, pumps and jackhammers.

<Four miners in pursuit,> said Smith. Freed from his holster, his eyepiece gave him a 360-degree view. <Check that,> he said. <Another elevator just opened. Now that's nine. Wait, there's a convoy approaching too.>

I wanted to shout *enough already*, but I needed to put my oxygen to better use. I sped as fast as my lungs would allow, taking turns as Smith called them out, the sound of approaching boots stampeding behind me.

<One more turn,> said Smith. <You see that ramp

coming up on the right? Take it down, and you'll find a set of stairs on the far side of a large room. The stairs lead to the access tunnel.>

I hit the ramp hard, ready for freedom, but my feet ground to a halt. The bottom half of the ramp was submerged in water. I couldn't see the staircase that led to the access tunnel. The room was flooded.

I shouted out loud, "SMITH!"

<Um, water wasn't on the map.>

Footsteps came close, and I ducked, a pickax whizzing past my head. Then another.

I spun and fired. A pulse of light rippled out of Smith. The six-shooter was a Moon family hand-me-down. I'd kept the frame but replaced the guts with a modern pulseripper.

The shot sliced through three miners, scattering their lifeless bodies across the floor. The others hustled for cover around the corner.

<I told you to stun, not kill!>

<I was protecting you, Denver.>

Rafe's head poked around the corner, and I forced him back with another pulse burst.

<Whatever. Just get us out of here. Fast.>

<This water must be runoff from a sluice.>

<I don't care where it came from. Can I swim it?>

<Yes. I see vertical vents big enough for you to fit into. Go under, and you can come up at each vent.>

<I sure as shit hope you saw air on that map of yours.>

I took one more shot before Smith transformed back into pistol mode and I shoved him into his holster.

And then I dove.

One rung after another, I climbed down the access ladder, the rusted safety cage scraping the back of my jacket. Wet pants chafed my thighs, and water squished in my boots. A wet shiver shook my spine. Damn that Rafe Ranchard.

Going back to the mine was out of the question. Same for calling the ministry. There were three dead miners now, but I had no doubt Rafe would keep quiet. The dirt I had on him would keep his mouth shut good and tight. And even if he did squeal, Smith's recording of the event would prove I acted in self-defense.

Rafe Ranchard was a score that needed settling, and settle it I would. But not today. Today, I had to swallow my pride no matter how bad it tasted.

Reaching the ladder's last rung, I hopped down to the ground. I ducked through a gap between vents to find the long, narrow corridor of the lower levs.

Mars City and most of its supporting installations and communities were located in the topmost levels. The less legitimate facilities and businesses sprouted below.

Not many people go deeper than Red Tunnel, and those who do sure don't want anybody knowing what they do in these parts: Things that can't be done even in the tawdriest corners of the tunnel.

Smith was on full alert and reacted at his own discretion, no orders necessary from me. He had led me here. By tapping into the cameras found outside the mine, he'd been able to track the suspicious pair of miners from camera feed to camera feed all the way to this corridor.

We were looking for a door. A special kind of door.

There are three kinds of doors in the lower levs. The first kind are simple ID-locked doors. Easy enough to get through, but solid enough to protect those on the inside from casual intruders.

The second kind have a more sophisticated system, backed up by another lock. These doors often hide people who want to lie low for a bit, get away from whatever heat was spreading their way uplev. The cases that brought me down here generally ended behind a type two door.

Type three are more secure, some of the doors flanked by botsie or human guards. This was where the lower lev royalty lived, the illegal pronoid manufacturers, the outlaw pharmakings, the people who sold the stuff that would make a botstringer like Jard Calder blush. Come across one of those, and Smith and I would give it a wide berth. I wouldn't take on one of those without a full squad of assault bots, and even then I'd give the matter a second thought.

It was a type two door Smith and I were looking for,

one that had two men inside. Smith was alert for their heat signatures.

I stopped to cough. I'd nearly drowned back there, and my lungs wheezed like water was still trapped inside.

<I'm sorry, Den,> said Smith.

<For what?>

<I underestimated the distance to that first air vent. I almost lost you.>

His voice was tinged with fear. He almost sounded concerned. Like Ojiisan had after I fell off of a grav-lift when I was a little girl. But Smith wasn't my grandfather. Just a clever piece of programming.

I stopped in front of a door. <Are you getting two heat signatures?>

<I said I was sorry, Denver. I need to know we're good.>

<Are you asking me to forgive you?>

<It would make me feel a lot better to know that you're not mad at me. I wouldn't ever knowingly put you in harm's way.>

I wanted to remind him of what he was. A program. And a program couldn't *feel*. Yet I knew he would keep harping on the issue until I gave him what he wanted.

<I forgive you,> I said with no emotion. <Now are you getting heat signatures or not?>

<No. Nothing.>

I moved to the next door.

<One human,> said Smith. I started toward the next door when he said, <And one bot.>

<So?>

<Might be somebody having a good time, but I'm also wondering if one of those two miners I tracked down here could've been a bot.>

<Bots don't do shift work in the mines.>

<True,> he said. <They work around the clock, and they don't get paid. But what if a bot was passing?>

Passing for human? This case just kept getting stranger.

I pulled Smith from his holster. <Pop the lock.>

I heard the click, and I stepped inside fast. I kicked the door shut behind me even as my eyes took in the grays of the one room hovel.

A startled man stood at an easel, old-style, using brushes and paint on a canvas. His nude model leaned against a wall. On the floor was a jumpsuit and a hooded jacket. Tools were stacked in the corner, a pickax resting among them.

The model was a male botsie. I could see that in the facial structure, but the rest of it was…changed. The left arm was slenderer than the right. Its torso bore breasts. Between the legs was female. The skin tones of the replaced parts didn't match, giving the bot a bizarre quilt-like quality.

"What did you do?" I said to the painter. My voice was harsh. "You got the feve?"

Before he could speak, another voice answered.

"He is doing this for me," the botsie said. "He's doing this because I asked him to help me."

The botsie moved slowly toward the painter as if unsteady on its new legs, and the painter positioned himself protectively between me and it, shielding the bot.

"Don't hurt her," he said, his voice as sharp as his eyes.

"Her?" I said. "Whatever you've done, and why ever you've done it, it's still a botsie. A male botsie. Those parts belong to Jard."

"She was never a male," he said. "Never completely. Never meant to be."

"Meant to be? Come on, you know better than that. Botsies are meant to be whatever they're programmed to be. Whatever Jard or any other 'stringer pays for them to be. They're built the way their owners want."

"I wasn't," the botsie said. Its voice was rich and calm. "I knew from the first moment I wasn't meant to be male. I was meant to be what I'm becoming now. What Stieg is helping me become. He's helping me become who I really am."

"You're a bot. Not a person."

"Something went…astray with her programming," Stieg said. "She was trapped in the wrong body. I'm helping her fix that."

"By taking apart other botsies? By destroying property belonging to Jard Calder?"

"I didn't destroy their chips." Stieg pointed to a jar on

the floor, a handful of chips inside. "I kept them intact. What I did was for a higher good."

"Tell that to the judge," I said.

"Don't do this," Stieg said, a note of fierceness in his tone. "They'll change Ana back to the way she was. She'd rather die than go back to living a lie."

"You may as well kill us now," said Ana.

"Kill you? You're a botsie. No killing involved."

"She's a living being," said Stieg. "She knows who she is, and all I have done is help her become herself. If you… if you knew her the way I do, you'd help her too."

"You're delusional."

"I love her," Stieg said, all the fierceness gone from his voice. "And she loves me."

I looked into Stieg's eyes. I saw something there, something he thought was love. Something I thought was the feve.

I couldn't look *into* the botsie's eyes, only *at* them, but something similar dwelled there.

"It can't love," I said.

"Yes," said Ana. "I can. I do."

"The other botsies," said Stieg, "they were her friends. She was a prostitute working the mines, and she became friends with Jard's bots who worked the same district. Her botstringer died, and he didn't will her to anybody, so she was free, understand? She was a free bot, maybe the only one on all of Mars. But she wasn't truly free, not as long as she was trapped in the wrong body. Her friends, they understood, and they offered to give up parts. I told them I'd take care of their chips and see to it they were reconstructed one day. We didn't do anything illegal. The bots volunteered."

"Why so many volunteers? Why not just one?"

"She needed to become entirely unique. Entirely *herself.* And her friends understood."

I listened to every word.

Their story sounded so. . .human. A part of me wanted to believe them. But I'd come here to do a job, and I wasn't going to get talked out of it no matter how much their story challenged my worldview.

"Let's go," I said. "I'm bringing you to Jard, and collecting my fees. You can work out the rest with him."

"No," said Stieg and Ana simultaneously. They held each other's hands.

"He'll change her back, and he'll make her prostitute herself. She won't live as a slave. You'll have to kill us," Stieg said.

Stieg's free hand went into his pocket.

"Let's not do anything stupid," I said.

Slowly, measuring my face all the while, Stieg pulled out a small mining tool and pressed a button to open the blade. Six inches of steel began to vibrate at jackhammer speed. Smith was an insistent pressure in my hand, but I didn't want to pull the trigger.

"Let's talk about this," I said.

"You going to let us go?"

"I can't do that."

Stieg lunged forward, and pulses of light rapid-fired from Smith. The bursts smashed both Stieg and the bot into the wall with a sickening thud.

I looked at Smith. I hadn't pulled the trigger.

<I got them, Denver,> he said.

<Dammit, Smith, I didn't want you to do that!>

<I had to protect you.>

I looked to the bodies. One was dead. The other shut down.

<I could've disarmed him. I could've convinced them to come with us.>

<That wasn't going to happen. They'd already decided to die for each other.>

<How could you know that?>

<You saw the way they looked at each other. They were in love.>

<What do you know of love?>

<I know I love you, Denver.>

I stared at what remained of Stieg and Ana. Their bodies were tangled together, Stieg's blood spreading over the botsie's torso, her bio-hydraulic fluid spreading over his. I dropped to the floor and leaned my back against the wall.

I didn't move for a long time, my brain knotting with confusion. It didn't have to go like that, dammit. But every time I played the scene through my head, no matter how I changed the script, it always ended the same way.

Stieg and Ana, their lifeless bodies in a twisted heap.

They looked the same now.

I couldn't tell the difference.

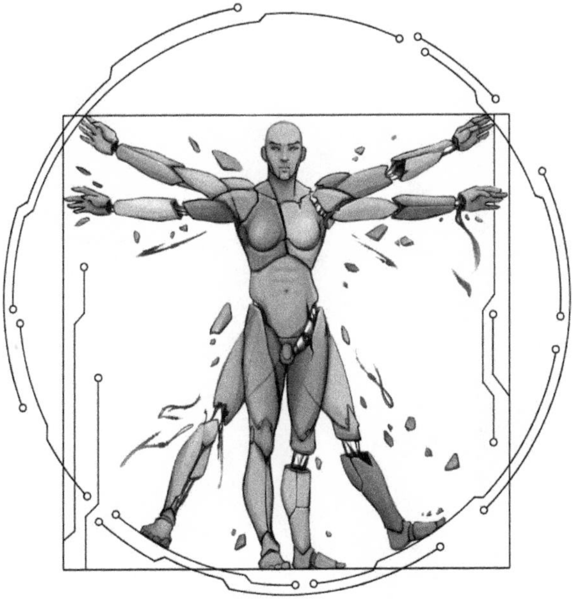

SNEAK PEEK

DENVER MOON: BOOK TWO

I KEPT TO THE SHADOWS, BACK PRESSED AGAINST the wall, my head swiveling left and right. Scanning. Searching.

Two months' work, and I finally had a name; Lucas Robbins. Aged 47. Earthborn. Immigrated to Mars six years back. Address unknown.

The market was busy this time of day. Shift changes up and down the levs crowded the tunnels of this ant colony of a city. Hawkers pitched their wares. Amplified by scratchy speakers, their garbled voices drilled into my ears. Cooks worked fryers and griddles inside cramped booths soaked in bright neon. Electric fans lured customers by blowing the enticing odors of spiced faux meat out into the thoroughfares.

The latest missing person had last been seen at the noodle bar down the way. That was two days ago. Two days since anybody had seen Millie Lopez, her last known meal a tofu bowl split between her and her mother, the noodle bar's prep cook.

A teenaged boy peeled off from the mass of people moving past. Approaching me, he touched a finger to the artery in his neck. I waved him away. Standing in the recesses like I was, he couldn't be the only one to mistake me for a quick-jab dealer.

<See anything, Smith?> I subvocalized to the AI installed in my gun.

<Facial rec still reporting no hits,> he said. <But I can't see very well from here. Even looking through your eyes I can only make out about half of the faces well enough for comparisons. Any way you can get me to a higher location?>

I pulled the Smith & Wesson off my belt and reached up to balance him atop a water pipe that ran the length of the wall.

<Turn me a little to the left, Denver, and move me closer to the edge.>

I complied, doing my best to give his visual sensors the broadest possible view while keeping the gun balanced on the rounded surface. <How's that?>

<Much better. Still can't see everybody, but I can see most as they pass.>

I arched my back and pressed my shoulders against the grimy wall. You'd think a sealed environment like the tunnels this far down would be spotless, but the dust from the terraforming project was an insidious bastard.

Try as we might to keep the whirling clouds of dust out, a fine, powdery grit still wormed its way through the filters, and along the corridors, and down the lifts and dropshafts, the stairwells and ladder tubes, to cover everything with a film I was told was red. I wouldn't know. All grit and grime is the same color to me, just like the people—the clothes they wear, the blood they spill. Other people see colors and shades. I just see Mars.

A headache started shoving at the backs of my eyes. I pushed harder against the rock wall. The kink between my shoulder blades didn't appreciate the pressure, but I pressed harder.

I needed a massage.

A three-day drunk or a four-day zone.

A month of sleep.

I needed another line of work, one that didn't have me tied up in knots and working around the clock. I needed a change of scenery, something other than endless corridors, featureless except for the conduits and pipes that carried power and water in, shit and piss out.

It started to rain.

That was what people called it anyway. I knew better.

It was recycled wastewater. Reclaimed piss from the people who lived in the surface domes up above our heads. Their piss wasn't any purer than ours, not before it was 'cycled anyway. And it didn't come down on *their* heads a couple of times a week in a futile attempt to rinse the grit from the walls and floors. They got real rain, or what passed for it on Mars—fresh water showers straight from the ice-claimers. Sweet and clear and unused for millions of years. Once their streets were clean and their gardens watered, it ran into the sewer tubes and through the 'cyclers before being piped down to us so we could pretend it was raining.

Mist filled the stale air, dewy drops gathering on the ceiling and walls. I'd never seen real rain, but I knew this wasn't it. Reminded me of an old joke Smith pulled from my grandfather's memories: <Don't piss on my boots and tell me it's raining.>

But that's just what the topsiders did, and up there in the clean air under the domes they told themselves they were doing us a favor, letting their wastewater trickle down on all us unfortunates in the corridors and caverns beneath them. Their kind had a history of trickling down, a history that went all the way back to Earth long before anybody had left it.

I rubbed the back of a hand against my eyes, wiping the water away.

<I got him,> Smith said.

I stood straight. Every nerve in my body began to tingle. For two months, I'd been working this dead end of a case. No evidence. No witnesses. No leads. Nothing at all until an hour ago.

I grabbed hold of Smith and thumbed off his safety. Taking a deep, wet breath, I stepped out of the shadows.

<Turn left,> whispered Smith.

The mist was coming down harder now, and I blinked against it as I stepped into the crowd.

<He's twenty feet ahead, Denver.>

I moved deeper into the promenade, the noodle bar to my right. I glanced through the window. The security cams hadn't shown anything out of the ordinary when Millie Lopez walked out the door for the last time, but a half hour earlier the feeds showed a man slurping noodles by himself. A hat and glasses hid much of his face, but Smith had more than enough to work with when he cross-checked the restaurant's clientele against all the other security feeds of the last-known locations of each of the nine people who had gone missing since I was hired.

Finally, we had a match. Lucas Robbins. He'd been spotted walking past the pharmapit our third missing person liked to frequent. No sign of Robbins at any of the other locations we'd catalogued, but two hits were enough to know he was our guy. Seeing as both the pharmapit and the noodle bar were in this same market area, I hoped he might pass through frequently, and now, just an hour later, I was on his tail. That was how cases went sometimes. Nothing for weeks or months at a time, then it came all at once.

I picked up my pace, closing the gap between me and him, my gun held low, where nobody would notice unless they were looking for it. <That him in the brown coat?>

<That's him.>

My finger quivered on the trigger, eager to drop him. But that wasn't the smart play. The smart play was to call the ministry of police, and let them take it from here. But my client insisted on keeping the cops out. Not an unusual request down here in the lower levs. In fact, I didn't even know who my client was. Requesting anonymity was also pretty damn common down in the bowels, and anonymity was a service I was happy to provide as long as they paid well, and on time.

I moved closer so that there were only a few feet between him and me. A quick pulse was all it would take to collapse him into a twitching heap. But there were nine people missing. I figured them all for dead, but as long as there was a chance any were still breathing, I needed to follow him instead.

The space seemed to narrow as we snaked through a group of Church of Mars monks proselytizing and begging for alms. The crowd tightened around me, and despite my best efforts, I fell behind, my eyes squinting through the mist, struggling to stay locked onto his tall, angular frame.

I shouldered my way through a knot of people just in time to see him leave the main promenade and enter an alley, the falling water making him blurry to my eyes.

Quickening my pace, I tightened my fingers around Smith's grip as I entered the alley. Jammed full of stalls and food stands, the alley only afforded a single-file path. Yet he was gone. No sign of my quarry.

<Dammit, where did he go?>

<I don't know.>

I marched up to the first food stand where soyakebabs sizzled on a flat grill, their sputtering and popping echoed by droplets dribbling down from the alley's roof.

The little man tending the grill grinned, but before he could launch into his sales pitch, I pointed my gun at his face. The guy's eyes grew wide, and he swayed like he was about to pass out.

<Show him,> I subvocalized.

From the top of the gun, Smith projected a small hologram of Lucas Robbins.

"You see this man?" I asked, my voice sounding rough and harsh. It'd been some time since I'd spoken out loud. "You see where he went?"

The guy shook his head and spread his arms wide, the oily spatula in his right hand dripping with grease. "No. I didn't see anybody. I was—"

"Don't give me that. He just walked past two seconds ago."

"Lots of people walk past. I was flipping my kebabs."

I turned away and blocked the path of a woman headed for the promenade. I held Smith out so she could see the holo shimmering in the falling mist. "Seen him?"

The woman shook her head, and I moved on.

The alley was a dead end. There were only so many places he could have gone, and I worked them as quickly as I could, but none of the vendors or their customers would admit to seeing him. I was nearly at the end of the short tunnel before I had any luck—a small voice saying, "I saw him."

I looked down.

A beggar girl wrapped in a dirty blanket sat with an alms-bowl on a filthy scrap of rug. She spoke again, her voice a little louder this time. "I saw him come right by here but he didn't pop me any credits or even slow down when I asked."

Her face was streaked and smeared from the mist and dust. Her eyes were large and dark. The combination ought to have been good for business, but there was nothing in her bowl.

"Where did he go?"

"Won't say—not unless I get paid."

I bit off a curse, dug deep into my jacket pocket and flipped her a handful of credits, some of which missed her bowl.

She gathered the credits, but even as she did, she nodded at the facade of the metalworks shop that capped the end of the alley. "He went in there," she said.

"There any other ways in or out?"

"Nope," she said, her attention still on the credits now gathered in the bowl.

I was about to thank her, but something held me back. Something was off. I kept my eye on her as I stepped toward the door of the metalworks shop.

I gripped my gun tight in my fist. <You ready, Smith?>

<I was initialized ready.> Another one of his bad jokes.

Reluctant to take my eyes off of the girl, I jerked open the door and was flooded with bright light and flashing beams of what I assumed were different hues, but it all just looked like light to my colorblind eyes. I checked on the girl again. She sat right where I left her, and I held my breath for a second before I went inside.

I looked for the proprietor or an attendant, but there was no one. A digital voice sounded from a speaker near the door. "Welcome. How can I help you?"

<Roboshop,> Smith said. <Odd.>

It was—who would finance a totally automated shop at the end of a third-class marketplace on a lower level? I filed that question away for later, and ignoring the house AI's repeating welcomes, I made a quick inspection of the place. Sparks showered from articulated welding lasers moving fast like spider legs. Near the door, boxes of cogs and circuit boards sat on shelves ready for pickup. Annealing guns and smelting pods blasted white-hot heat that made my damp clothes tighten around me.

<You sense any humans?> I asked Smith.

<Scans say not a one.>

I sighed heavily and ran my eyes around the shop one more time, my gaze coming to a section of bricks set into the wall. <You see that?>

<See what?>

I stepped up to the wall. <See how the mortar doesn't match?>

<No. Let me patch in to your eyes.>

I ran my fingertips over the mortar.

<I see it now,> said Smith. <Too much light pollution for me to see it with my own sensors.>

It didn't happen often, but every once in a while, my monochrome vision picked up something others couldn't see. Tracing the irregular trail of mortar with my fingers, I followed the line all the way down to the floor, where the lowest brick gave slightly beneath my touch. I pushed harder and the wall shifted, sliding aside to reveal a narrow, dark corridor cut through stone.

That sneaky bastard.

<Make yourself a little more intimidating,> I told Smith.

<Cannon mode?>

<No. Just a holo for now, we don't know what we're going to find. But make it a *scary* holo.>

Smith glowed for an instant and the gun's sleek lines disappeared beneath a hologram overlay that doubled its size and sprouted big over/under barrels and a balloon magazine.

<Bigger,> I said.

Smith shimmered again and blossomed into a now triple-barreled weapon, belt-fed, with alternating explosive and penetration cartridges. He projected a long bandolier of cartridges that stretched up to drape over my shoulders.

<Happy now?> Smith said with a touch of impatience.

<Nice,> I said. <Let's go.>

I was four steps into the tunnel when I heard the wall slide shut behind me. I didn't look back. Smith bloomed a lightstalk and the tunnel ahead glowed softly. I took three more steps and heard the wall behind me slide open again.

I looked over my shoulder to see the beggar girl, her features cold and angry now. In a flash, I knew what bothered me about her. Her alms bowl had no water in it. She must have just arrived in the alley when she claimed to see Robbins.

I'd barely started to dive for cover when she pulled the trigger of the gun she held in her hand.

Her gun was smaller than Smith, even without the holo projections, but it was big enough to fill the tunnel with nova-bright light that struck me hard and left me unconscious on the floor.

I was so cold. My teeth chattered uncontrollably, and my shoulders quaked. My vision was blurred and my thoughts weren't any clearer. The pain between my shoulder blades had turned into an unrelenting agony, like it was about to pull me apart. I closed my eyes and drew a deep breath of stale air thick with the smell of copper. I held it long enough for my vision to begin to sharpen.

My hands were tied together, tight, and the cord that bound my wrists was looped over a metal hook that might've been fabricated in the robotic metalshop that fronted this place, whatever this place was.

Other bodies hung from identical hooks, but none of their hands—those that still had them—were tied. Instead, their arms hung limp and lifeless by their sides. Some of the corpses had been decapitated, neck stumps protruding from sagging shoulders. Others still had their heads, but the tops of their skulls had been removed like lids from jars. Hoisted and impaled, their chests were pierced by sharp points. I held my breath again and looked down.

My feet dangled maybe twenty inches off the ground. The floor was dark with splotches and stains of blood. Long gutters carved into the stone ran to a large floor drain.

<For exsanguination,> Smith said.

Smith lay on a low metal table in front of me. A man's body lay beside him. <Exsangui— what?>

<Exsanguination. Bleeding out. You see the shunts inserted into the arteries in their thighs and wrists? They're used to let the blood drain out.>

<Great.>

<I've been trying to call for help, but this place must be shielded. I can't get any kind of signal. You need to find a way out of here, Denver.>

<No shit.> I tried to flex my fingers but I couldn't feel them. <I'm freezing. How long have I been hanging here?>

<Two hours and—>

<Long enough,> I said. <How many bodies can you see?>

<Dozens.>

Dozens? I shouldn't have been surprised the number was so much larger than the nine I knew of. The lower levs were crammed with lost souls who would never be missed.

Shivers shook my spine and rattled my teeth. It was damn cold in here. I lifted my legs, then dropped them back down to get a small swing started. Screaming shoulders told me to stop, but I swung again, creating a wider arc. If I built up enough momentum, maybe I could get the cord linking my wrists off the hook.

A door slid open and the beggar girl came through. The blanket she'd had wrapped around her shoulders in the alley was gone. Her brown jacket hung so loose, I realized it had been fitted for a grown man. Same for the pant legs that bunched around her ankles. She studied me for a moment, her large eyes moving slowly back and forth with the rhythm of my body. She shook her head and approached.

I prepared to kick her as hard as I could but she kept out of range and came in from behind before grabbing my legs. Her powerful grip dug painfully into the backs of my thighs, and she brought my swings to a stop. "Don't try that again," she said. Her voice was strong, no sign of the waif she'd played in the marketplace.

She stepped to the table where Smith lay beside the corpse. For a moment she didn't move, but then her eyes closed, and she shivered gently before seeming to grow taller. I blinked to shake away what must have been a hallucination, but she continued to grow. The baggy-fitting brown jacket began to fill out, and under the fabric of the sleeves, I saw arms stretching until fingers and hands emerged from the cuffs. Her face became more masculine, soft cheekbones hardening while her brow bulged to cut a sharp line over her eyes.

"Robbins," I said, my voice a hoarse croak.

<He's an alien,> Smith said into my head.

I knew the bugs could take human form, but shapeshifting in a matter of seconds was a new trick, one that filled my stomach with dread. How were we supposed to stop them when they could pretend to be anybody they liked? Maybe my grandfather was right. We couldn't hope to defeat them. One way or the other, we were destined to be their slaves.

The shapeshifter strapped the corpse's head to the table with metal bands, and arranged an array of tools and implements on the table's surface. When he was satisfied, he looked back at me, his eyes bright.

"I have a bit of work to do here," he said, "and thought you might appreciate seeing the process before it's applied to you. Actually," he corrected, "in your case, it might be necessary to perform my duties upon a *living* specimen."

"Lucky m-me," I said, shivering so bad it was a struggle to get the words out. "What is this p-place?"

He looked at my gun, his good fortune that the barrel was pointing the other way. "An Earth shooter, yes? Smith & Wesson, I believe, referred to in antiquity as a six-shooter. Of course, yours isn't entirely antique, is it? The holographic projection you installed was most impressive."

<He'll be more impressed if you can get a shot at him, Smith.>

<Believe me, Denver, I will as soon as I get the opportunity. As long as he doesn't know about me, we have a chance.>

"So w-what is this place?" I asked again, speaking as loud and tough as I could manage hanging from a hook with my hands numb and tied above my head. "You work for D-doctor Werner?"

The shapeshifter's attention turned on me, and Smith rotated his cylinder by one. In the process, his barrel turned a few degrees in the right direction. A half dozen more cylinder rotations and he might have a shot.

"You know my associate is g-going to come looking for m-me," I said while Smith made another rotation, the click covered by my voice. "He knows w-where I am."

"Excellent. I have an empty hook with his name on it."

Smith rotated again.

"You won't be able to run your s-sick experiments on him. H-he's an android."

Another rotation.

"Their skulls open just as easy," the shapeshifter said as he lifted a circular saw and brought the device to life with a high-pitched whine. He bent over the corpse's head. The room filled with the thrum of metal cutting through flesh and bone. Loud enough to cover Smith putting the cylinder through two more rotations before the shapeshifter shut off the saw and stepped back to survey his work.

As long as he was looking at the skull, I let my eyes flick back and forth between him and Smith, measuring the angle of the gun barrel and calculating the odds.

<Two more. Two more and you've got him.>

The shapeshifter peeled the top of the corpse's skull back and cracked it free.

He aimed a sick grin at me. "I wonder what the inside of your head looks like."

Smith moved partway through another cylinder click, but stopped when the shapeshifter glanced in his direction. The alien's eyes pinched a bit when he must have noticed that the gun's aim had turned on its own. I held my breath, hoping he'd assume the table vibrations caused by the sawing made the gun move.

He tossed the skullcap toward a garbage can and it struck the wall with a wet slap before falling into the pail.

<I'm so close,> said Smith. <I almost have him.>

<On three,> I said. I counted the digits for him, then screamed as loud as I could.

Startled, the shapeshifter jumped back and turned toward me as Smith put himself through two more quick rotations.

The shapeshifter took a step toward me before—

Smith took a shot.

Best he could under the circumstances, but not good enough. The pulse sailed wide and shredded two of the hanging corpses, leaving tattered body parts swinging wildly from their hooks. Meanwhile, the kickback from the discharge sent Smith skittering along the table, his cylinder spinning as he tried to line his barrel up for another shot.

The alien lunged for the table. Smith fired again. Another miss, but this one was close enough to drive the 'shifter back toward me just as I bent at the waist and lifted my legs high and wide. I brought them down over the shapeshifter's shoulders, hooking my knees under his arms, my thighs locked tight around his neck as I furiously levered us both backwards.

Swinging, his added weight made my arms feel like they were about to pull from their sockets. Gathering his feet underneath, he raised his arms and slipped free of my hold. Swinging forward now, I summoned all the strength I had to yank on my restraints, lifting myself high enough that my head bumped the metal hook. Waiting for my swing to hit its apex, I jumped the cord off the hook. Airborne, I collided with one of the hanging corpses before tumbling hard to the floor.

The shapeshifter rushed the table again, giving Smith only enough time to fire once more. The pulse plowed through another corpse before the table toppled, dissection tools scattering across the floor. I got to my feet and staggered after the alien, but I was too slow. He grabbed Smith and pointed the barrel at my head.

"W-wrong move," I said through chattering teeth.

The instant those words left my mouth, Smith let loose an electric charge strong enough to spin the shapeshifter around and drop him screaming and twitching to the floor, releasing the gun.

I picked up Smith with both of my bound hands, barely able to feel his familiar weight in my numb fingers.

<Cut me loose,> I said, breathing hard.

Smith extruded a small blade and sliced through cords that bound my wrists. I shifted him to my left hand and flexed the fingers of my right, my fingertips burning with the return of circulation.

I took a step toward the shapeshifter, who was still twitching. I knelt and put Smith's muzzle against his temple.

The shapeshifter trembled and became the beggar girl once more, staring up at me with the imploring eyes of a child who'd done wrong.

"Don't move," I said while my mind scrambled to decide on my next course of action. I wanted to question her for a long, painful time, but I couldn't be sure there weren't more of them down here somewhere. I thought about turning her over to the authorities, but she was an alien, and aliens were a secret. If word got out that they existed and were running our terraforming project, the delicate balance that kept this world inching toward a viable future would be destroyed.

She made up my mind for me when she grabbed a scalpel from the floor. I squeezed Smith's trigger and let him take off the top of her head.

Smith was neither as neat nor as precise as the shapeshifter had been with his saw, but he got the job done. Bits of bone and brain, or whatever the bugs called it, splattered across the room. Black goo blew back to spray my hands and arms.

The alien shifted once again. Flesh and muscle melted into chitinous legs and arms. A sectioned body showed through his shirt. His neck, long and narrow, led to a mantis-like head, what was left of it.

<Nice shooting,> Smith said as I raised his muzzle toward my mouth. He projected a holo of gun smoke and I pursed my lips to blow it away.

I stood and stretched my tingling arms. Again, I looked around this horror show of a space, and seeing so many people hanging like slabs of meat, any urge to celebrate further quickly faded.

The alien didn't move. I figured it for dead, but I'd once seen one of them recover from a broken spine, so who was to say blowing their brains out counted as a kill shot?

<Denver?>

<What, Smith?>

<You see the top of the spinal column?>

I bent down to look inside the cranial cavity. <I guess so.>

<I just scanned it. Same for the chunk of brain that's still there.>

<And?>

<I think it's human.>

DENVER WILL RETURN

www.DenverMoon.net

DENVER
MOON
READ THE GRAPHIC NOVEL
METAMORPHOSIS
HAMMOND ▾ LOVETT ▾ VIOLA

ABOUT THE AUTHORS

Warren Hammond grew up in the Hudson River Valley of New York State. Upon obtaining his teaching degree from the University at Albany, he moved to Colorado, and settled in Denver where he can often be found typing away at one of the local coffee shops.

Warren is known for his gritty, futuristic *KOP* series. By taking the best of classic detective noir, and reinventing it on a destitute colony world, Warren has created these uniquely dark tales of murder, corruption and redemption. *KOP Killer* won the 2012 Colorado Book Award for best mystery.

Warren's last novel, *Tides of Maritinia*, released in December of 2014. His first book independent of the *KOP* series, *Tides* is a spy novel set in a science fictional world.

Along with his critique partners, Warren co-hosts the popular CriTiki Party podcast.

Always eager to see new places, Warren has traveled extensively. Whether it's wildlife viewing in exotic locales like Botswana and the Galapagos Islands, or trekking in the Himalayas, he's always up for a new adventure.

Joshua Viola is an author, artist, and former video game developer (*Pirates of the Caribbean, Smurfs, TARGET: Terror*). In addition to creating a transmedia franchise around *The Bane of Yoto*, honored with more than a dozen awards, he is the author of *Blackstar*, a tie-in novel based on the discography of Celldweller. His debut horror anthology, *Nightmares Unhinged*, was a *Denver Post* and Amazon bestseller and named one of the Best Books of 2016 by Kirkus Reviews. His second anthology, *Cyber World* (co-edited by Jason Heller), was an Independent Publisher Book Awards winner and Colorado Book Award finalist and named one of the Best Books of 2016 by Barnes & Noble. His short fiction has appeared in The Rocky Mountain Fiction Writers' *Found* anthology (RMFW Press), *D.O.A. III – Extreme Horror Collection* (Blood Bound Books), and *The Literary Hatchet* (PearTree Press). He lives in Denver, Colorado.